INNATRAEA

Novella Three: Road to Bethseda

E.R. ZAUGG

Innatraea@gmail.com

ISBN: (EBook) 979-8-89893-000-4

ISBN: (Paperback) 979-8-89893-001-1

ISBN: (Hardback) 979-8-89893-002-8

Library of Congress Control Number:

Any references to historical events, real people, or real places are used fictitiously. Names, characters, and places are products of the author's imagination.

Front cover image by E.R. Zaugg.

Book design by E.R. Zaugg

Printed by Innatraea LLC, in the United States of America.

First printing edition 2026

https://www.innatraea.com/

This book is dedicated to my child Siri.

I hope that you find the power of weaving dreams with your creativity, as you have taught me.

NORDRIA
KIEVAN
RENOWHN
TRIBELANDS
AEDONIA
ANDALUS
Desert Mountains
SOPHENE
THAVA
Porto de la Luce
BETHSEDA
Tal'bessa's Crossing
The Shepherd King
Hayersfjord
Farnhold
Allelle Falls
Moon Mountains
IMPERIAL SHINODA
Sea of Grass
TURSIM
The Tanglewood
ROYAL SEYLA
KINRAI
ARA'AYIM ISLES
FARUN DA'AI
Skywall
FARUNDIA
SCEOTAN
Djelem'den
Bay of Sivani
AMNG'KHOR
TEOKAHL
INNATRAEA
0   200   400   600   800   1000
Miles

Porto de la Luce
Daphshire
River of Kings
Old Cathyor
Brynn
BETHSEDA
RENOWHN TRIBELANDS
AEDONIA
Geisterschwert Family Farm
Gwyn Wood
Talberston's Crossing
Mu'ul Mountains
Pitceg River
The Shepherd King
Haversfjord
IMPERIAL SHINODA
The King's Highway
Farmhold
Renfal Forest
Aliselle Falls
River of Flowers
ROYAL SEYLA

Table of Contents:

"Gallwch chi golli brwydrau neu ryfeloedd, ond
peidiwch byth â gadael i'ch calon gael ei threchu.

You can lose battles or wars,
but never let your heart be defeated."

-Old Cathyoran Saying

PROLOGUE:
GWYNTOEDD ANSICR
(UNCERTAIN WINDS)

About eighteen years ago...

Gregoire D'Arganse, High King of Aedonia, held the relic up to the light of one of his small study's candles. The relic felt strange, its touch a sharp pang, as if judging him for sins he couldn't name. It was fashioned from the bones of some ancient beast and encased a bundle of what looked like long, petrified fangs. "This thing, will it accomplish what I need?"

Inquisitor Durand nodded, looking serious as always. "Yes. The detestable godless witch who gave it to me swore it would."

Durand shuddered, dry washing his hands, as though he were scrubbing off filth. "It came from Djelem'den's depths, wrested from the Weavers at great cost." Gaining control of himself, he crossed his arms and slipped his hands into the voluminous sleeves of his white robes. "Once activated, it will sever Trefn Cyfiawnder's connection to their Dryads, rendering their magic useless. I believe it can work for nearly a league. It will break them."

Gregoire slammed the relic down, shaking off its judging sting. Aedonia was his kingdom, and it was their right to conquer. War always exacted a cost, even if that price meant dealing with the godless.

He looked at Durand while rubbing his chin in thought. The man was far from his favorite Inquisitor. There was cruelty in him, a deep hunger cloaked in faith, wielded like a shield. Then again, that was the nature of all Jhorian Inquisitors; they earned their more common name, Crows, long ago. He didn't particularly like them, especially this one, but the Jhorian faith's cruel anointed served him well, allies despite their methods.

"How do we activate it?"

"With blood, Your Majesty." Durand stepped closer and pointed a long, pale finger at the sharp spines within the relic's core. "One must prick their finger on the thorns."

Gregoire nodded. It made sense. Most godless witchery required blood or sacrifice. "We will need to test it."

Durand's lips curled into a thin, humorless smile. "Yes. Though I believe these plans represent the Will of Jhoras, a test would be prudent."

Gregoire nodded and looked toward the door of his study. "Stanislav!"

The commander entered immediately, shoving the study's door out of his way, as if it were an enemy barricade. He was overzealous, but Gregoire often found that useful.

"Yes, Majesty?"

"Find several of your best men. I have a special mission for you that will require delicacy."

Stanislav saluted, placing a hand on his sword pommel. "Of course, Majesty, anything you need."

Gregoire motioned toward the relic. "Take this thing. Its abilities need to be tested." He refused to refer to magic. "Inquisitor Durand will accompany you, both to observe the results and show you how to activate it." Gregoire placed both hands on his desk and took on an even more serious demeanor. "Speak to no one of the results, save myself."

Stanislav stepped up to the desk. "Yes, Majesty. I will do as you command and remain quiet." He reached for the relic.

Gregoire blocked the man's arm and met his eyes. "Find a box to carry it in. Holding it is... unpleasant."

Stanislav's jaw tightened as he glanced at the relic. His eyes flickered with unspoken questions, but he knew better than to speak. "Yes, Your Majesty, right away." He pivoted and left the study. The man was loyal.

Gregoire turned to Durand. "He will get the task done. Make sure to find one of the Trefn Cyfiawnder witches for the testing. That is the only way we can be sure it works."

"Your Majesty is wise, as always."

Gregoire dismissed him with a nod. "Now leave me. I need to think."

Durand left without another word, quietly closing the door behind him. Gregoire opened the study window and returned to his desk. Fresh air always helped him think more clearly.

For years, he had never been able to plan an open confrontation with Cathyor. Though small, the kingdom wielded an advantage unlike any other: the godless witches of Trefn Cyfiawnder. Those damned women and their abilities—again refusing to acknowledge it as magic—counted for thousands of swords in battle, making them an unstoppable force. But if he could sever that advantage? The eastern kingdoms would finally be his.

He unrolled a tactical map of Cathyor, the most accurate depiction his cartographers could produce, and laid it out on his desk. Opening his small box of miniatura he kept nearby, he began arranging them in a divining game of war.

A sharp breeze swept through the window and knocked over his personal miniatura. Gregoire righted it immediately, but his hand lingered, fingertips brushing the faces of his lost family—brothers fallen. It would all be over soon, with this last bloody campaign. He reached for the next miniatura in his box.

It was time to plan.

. . . . . .

A few weeks later, Durand was walking his horse past the anointed and then the common Aedonian soldiers, guiding the animal slowly with his knees. The beast had no name, none he knew, anyway. What was the point of naming a single tool, when you had so many others? Names have power that tools did not need.

The men had apprehended one of the Trefn Cyfiawnder witches this morning; she'd been on patrol alone. The superstitious would give credence to luck, but Durand knew the Will of Jhoras when he saw it. He suppressed a wince as the cloth he used to clean his forearm caught the edge of his new wound. The cut had been necessary to activate the relic, and he'd wanted to test it himself.

Stanislav resisted handing it over at first. The man had been ordered by his king to perform this test and was told that Durand was only there to instruct and observe the results. But the use of power required Jhoras's hand. Once they'd left Bethseda, and the man realized Durand's anointed outnumbered his own men two to one, convincing him to hand over the relic had proven much easier than expected, given the man's original protestations. Fear was a great motivator, and one Durand had learned how to use at a very young age. The situation was now much more tenable.

Now the relic, and the box it had been placed inside of, rested within Durand's satchel. High King Gregoire had been correct: Holding the relic was indeed uncomfortable. He shuddered at the memory, tucking the blood-stained cloth beside that same box. He would keep it for later; it might hold secrets beyond the relic—blood shed through magic often did. The initial results exceeded his expectations. Durand had been nearly a league away from their target when he'd cut himself to activate the relic, yet his anointed had reported its effect almost immediately.

Everything would have to be carefully verified; however, dealing with godless relics required caution. Further study would be needed, and he'd make sure that his order had the task, since the relic was in his hands now.

Durand dismounted, brushing off his wound's sting—Jhoras's Will outweighed discomfort.

"Unhand me dogs!"

Durand smiled at the panic in the godless Trefn Cyfiawnder witch's voice. The very fact she was being held down by his anointed, while her now useless "magic" sword lay on the ground next to her, was evidence enough the relic worked. But he had to push her to make sure it could truly contain her. Innatraeans were their strongest toward the end, a lesson he had learned when first becoming an Inquisitor so many years ago.

As Durand neared her, he noticed she was younger than he had expected—perhaps a new recruit. He also noticed there was no Catena covering her eyes. The anointed used those veils to suppress magic; that none was needed here was further proof the relic worked.

Durand drew one of the Sica, Jhoras's divine dual-edged daggers, he kept at his waist as he stopped above her. The ceremonial daggers were blessed by Jhoras, and every anointed carried at least one. The look of pure terror in her eyes brought a pleasant smile to his face.

"Now then, witch, the real test." He smiled as she tried to break free again, arching her back with the effort. Durand kicked her now useless sword away and knelt by her. "It was unwise of you to be so far from your godless sisters. I am afraid your death will not be a merciful one. Jhoras has decreed your sins unforgiven, and has requirements of you."

Durand smiled while he leaned over her and slowly pushed his Sica into the ground near her eyes. The witch traced the movement, watching the blade glide past her face. She flinched in pure terror, eyes widening as a drop of his blood landed on her.

Durand took the bloodied cloth out and very gently wiped away the tears streaming down her face. Her eyes widened at the sight of the blood, her body trembling with fear. Pain was nowhere near as effective a tool as terror.

Durand glanced at her hands. Seeing one of them flexing feebly, trying to reach for her sword, he looked further away at the blade. It wasn't moving. Her magic would not help her now; her Dryad was gone.

Durand turned back to her and smiled at the look of terrified despair in her eyes. The relic worked. The godless witch had no power left, and she knew it. Durand pulled his Sica out of the ground as she closed her eyes, giving up on life. It was over now. He knew what he'd come here to learn. He looked at the men with him. "Do what you want with her. Make sure she's nice and pretty for her sisters to find."

A sharp breeze blew past him while they dragged her away, as if the forest itself was mourning.

. . . . . .

A few days later...

Cormac pushed the balcony doors open and closed his eyes, inhaling deeply, enjoying the fresh air and bright sunlight on his face. It was chilly outside, but the air would do his newly born son good. Prince Cian, their new baby boy, started crying, and it was the most glorious sound Cormac had ever heard. He looked back at the royal bed, and smiled, as his beautiful Isolde leaned down to kiss their baby on the head.

She looked up and met his eyes, and in them joy and love sparkled brightly. She nuzzled their son, her expression tender. He knew she would be upset once everything settled down, because she hadn't given birth to a daughter—though she would never speak of it. Isolde was a woman of pure love and respect. It was a great honor for the women of Trefn Cyfiawnder to have a daughter first, and she would always carry that in her heart.

Cormac loved her beyond reason and wished he could have spared her that pain. But his son still made them both smile, which was happiness enough for now. Prince Cian would solidify House Ahearne's reign by virtue of inheritance, which gave Cormac joy as a father and a king. He smiled, knowing they would try again. There were many children in their future, and by Rhiannon, most would be girls. Cathyor, as a kingdom, was ruled by its king, but the real power behind their people was the women of Trefn Cyfiawnder.

Their family biume Brianna sat by the bed, tending to Isolde and Cian, her eyebrows arched.

Cormac smiled sheepishly. "The fresh air will do my son good."

Brianna's eyebrows lifted, though the woman didn't speak.

Cormac laughed. "I know, I know. You're still the same woman who paddled my backside as a child."

As Cormac turned to close the balcony doors, a cold wind blew over him, piercing his tunic and making him shiver. He shrugged it off and latched the doors.

Both women laughed at him, to which he just smiled. These were the two most important women in Cormac's life, and they both loved him.

A soft knock came at their bedchamber door.

Brianna made to stand, but Cormac waved the woman back to her seat. "I'll answer it. I may be king, but I can do some things myself, and they need you more than I do."

She sat back down and leaned in to dote upon baby Cian.

When Cormac opened the door, he was greeted by Elspeth Anwyl, her hand resting on the pommel of the sword at her waist. She nodded— the only salute he required, which she knew well.

Elspeth had been amongst his royal guard, Gwarchodlu Brenhinol, for a number of years now, and he trusted her implicitly, which is why she was here today: for the symbolic honor of guarding their son's birth. He recently remembered hearing that she was now romantically involved with one of their soldiers. He wanted to ask her about it, and make sure the soldier was a good man, but at the moment, her usual smiling face was somber, her eyes and voice both shaken. "Majesty, I am afraid I have been given ill news. One of our sisters, she..."

Cormac held up a hand, interrupting her. He looked back at his wife and newly born son, basking in their warm glow. Bad tidings had no place here, not on this day. He gestured toward the antechamber, wordlessly instructing Elspeth to step back.

But of course, Isolde had a different opinion. "My mind's still sharp. Let her in, my love."

Cormac nodded and silently stood aside. As a man of Cathyor, even as their king, he understood that certain matters belonged to the women of Trefn Cyfiawnder. That was simply the way of things.

Elspeth walked past him and knelt beside the bed, lowering her head as she placed her hand on the pommel of her sword. "Sister, it's Ailbhe. They..." She choked and wiped tears from her eyes. "A patrol found her this morning. She's been taken from us. Someone has killed our sister."

Shock and heartbreak swept Isolde's face. The women of Trefn Cyfiawnder were unilaterally respected everywhere they went inside of Cathyor's borders. This was a tragedy that was unheard of, and worse, Ailbhe was Isolde's distant cousin.

Ailbhe's face flashed across Cormac's mind. She had been such a kind child and had only recently become a full sister of Trefn Cyfiawnder. The memory made him want to kill whoever was responsible with his bare hands. His hands clenched into fists and he stepped closer to Isolde.

She sat up and quietly handed Cian to Brianna's waiting arms. Cormac offered his hand. She didn't speak to him, but her hand gripped his in a way that indicated both her gratitude and loving respect. With his help, she knelt by Elspeth, and the women embraced, touching their foreheads together.

Isolde's voice shook with emotion. "What happened to my cousin?"

Elspeth startled back in shock. "Your cousin? I am so sorry, I did not know."

Isolde laid a hand on Elspeth's cheek. "It's alright. What happened to our sister?"

Elspeth rested her head on Isolde's shoulder as Isolde drew her closer, one hand coming to rest on the back of her head. "She was dismembered. Nailed to a tree."

Isolde gasped. "Rhiannon, preserve us. Who did this? How?"

Elspeth looked toward Cormac, her expression weighing whether it was wise to speak the next part in his presence or not.

Isolde squeezed her shoulder gently. "He's my husband and our king. It's alright. Speak."

Cormac shivered, wondering what matter was so dire. It must be ill tidings, indeed.

Elspeth choked but sat back up and wiped her eyes before meeting Isolde's gaze. "There is more. Her magic, it didn't work. Her Dryad was there weeping when they found our sister, saying she couldn't feel Ailbhe when it happened."

Cormac shook with uncertainty and rage. Ill tidings, indeed. Every woman of Trefn Cyfiawnder was bonded to a Dryad, the magical titans of nature who gave the women their magic and purpose.

Isolde's eyes took on an inner fury. "Who did this and how?"

Elspeth sat up, her eyes wet but steady. "We don't know. Gwendolyn has dispatched Cysgod to investigate."

Cormac nodded to himself silently. The Cysgod would hunt for the truth.

"That is well. Gwendolyn knows what she is doing. I'll speak to her." Isolde's eyes grew more compassionate as she hugged Elspeth again.

"They brought my cousin—" There was a pause in Isolde's speech. "—our sister—back home?"

Elspeth's voice shook with anger and sadness. "Yes, she is home."

Isolde stroked the other woman's hair. "Rhown ein chwaer i orffwys, bydded iddi gael heddwch yn y Byd Nesaf." *We will lay our sister to rest, may she find peace in the next world.*

She looked at Cormac. "I don't care if you must carry our royal bed outside. I will go to my sisters. They need me. We must honor Ailbhe and find out what happened."

Cormac didn't argue. There was no point. This was his duty, and theirs. He also couldn't help but feel a chill deep in his bones, as he wondered what this meant for all their futures.

If the women of Trefn Cyfiawnder were no longer safe, then what did that mean for Cathyor? A gust of wind rattled the latched balcony doors, as if in answer.

Chapter One:
Brenhines yn Sefyll
(A Queen Stands)

"Marw yn dda chwaer, oherwydd buoch fyw yn ddewr.
Die well sister, for you have lived with courage."
-Trefn Cyfiawnder Farewell

A year later...

Isolde stared out of the large throne room's balcony windows. It had been nearly a year since her cousin Ailbhe's death. Her failed magic haunted Isolde. The Cysgod's lone warning of a thorned artifact had vanished with them. Now Brynn, her beloved city, her people's capital, was burning, and with it her kingdom.

Though a storm begun as afternoon came, it was too late to save them. Lightning and thunder crashed as rain fell over the flaming debris of her childhood home. Isolde spoke in the old tongue, her people's language, even though there was no one to hear it. She needed to say farewell to them in her heart and wish them safe passage. "Marw yn dda fy mhobl, oherwydd buoch fyw yn ddewr, ffarwel. Boed i chi ddod o hyd i heddwch yn y Byd Nesaf." Die well my people, for you have lived with courage, farewell. May you find peace in the next world.

There was not much left now, but a few things she could still do. Her son—and as many of her sisters in Trefn Cyfiawnder as possible—would survive. She would see to that before her death: A few last glimmers of hope. A queen stood. It was the Cathyoran way. She would take as many of their enemies with her as she could into Byd Nesaf. She was Cathyor's queen, and her magic still worked. There would be no mercy for their enemy's souls.

Isolde turned around as she heard them coming for her. The main throne room had open arches, and the invaders were loud with their lust for destruction. It had taken some argument to convince Cormac leave her here alone. But he also had a duty to fulfill, and she was a warrior. He knew better than to deny her this. She said a silent prayer to Rhiannon and drew her sword, whose name was Cynddaredd, or "Fury," into her hand, dropping its scabbard to her side as they entered the large room.

Something unknown and deadly had sealed much of their magic away when the invasion had started, but Isolde was their queen, the strongest of them. Cynddaredd's blade seethed with the crackling dark amber lightning of its hunger, wanting to devour her enemies as she raised it in challenge. "Vermin! Come meet your end!"

There was an Inquisitor with them—there always was when they were spreading the "Will" of Jhoras. He stepped forward from the ranks of knights and soldiers as their archers ran upstairs to the upper balconies. She didn't know this one's name, but he clearly thought himself clever, confident he could handle her. He looked around the throne room in an almost leisurely manner and smiled. "Is that any way to address the anointed of Jhoras?"

Isolde's face hardened. She could feel her anger boiling deep inside, like heartbreak turned into a sword blade. "You call yourselves anointed and speak of faith? How many women and children have died at your hands today, Inquisitor? You are nothing but a common dog. You and all of your men are nothing but criminals and murderers!"

He gently touched the three-quarter Jhorian cross hanging around his neck and smiled almost kindly; the contrast of his expression to his words was sickening. "I am Inquisitor Durand. Though you may see things differently, Innatraeans who live in sin must be granted the Lord's Mercy. It is just." He met her eyes, and all she saw in them was madness. "You however were a queen, and I will be kind. You may surrender now and your mercy will be painless."

She smiled wickedly and raised Cynddaredd a touch higher. "I am still a queen more so than you will ever understand. Your death shall not be a quiet or merciful one. Come, Inquisitor, and face your end."

"Very well, godless witch. I offered you kindness, and you spat on it." Durand grinned wickedly and twitched his fingers ever so slightly. The archers on both sides of the balcony fired.

Isolde swept Cynddaredd through the air. The sword felt the threat to her life, and its magic reacted. Dark amber lightning lashed out, burning the arrows to cinders and seeking those who had sent them. The archers screamed in pain, almost as one, while they died burning. She made eye contact with Inquisitor Durand and took a step forward. "I am no easy prey, you sanctimonious bastard. Come, I have my own version of mercy in mind for you."

Durand tilted his head, unfazed. "I heard the Trefn Cyfiawnder queen witch was powerful. How interesting." He nodded calmly to his men. "Kill the godless witch."

The soldiers surged toward her, blades gleaming as the storm outside increased in rage, seeming to feel her people's loss and anger. That raging hatred and sadness echoed itself in her Cynddaredd, as the lightning on its blade grew more erratic, sparking with its hunger. Isolde charged forward, not waiting for them to come, but going to meet their crazed destruction with the anger of her despair. Her blade arced. Lightning flowed behind it, seeking prey. Where she blocked or struck, it sparked along the metal of their weapons and armor, burning those inside with its fiery magic. They weren't ready for her. They had not expected this, and it was over quickly, but the ending was not one she had expected.

As the last one screamed, dying in pain, instinct told her to strike to her left, and there Cynddaredd's blade met a low stroke from the twin daggers wielded by Inquisitor Durand. Her sword's lightning did not arc along those cruel-looking blades to his flesh, but instead sprang away from him and disappeared. Isolde felt something like a spike or thorn pushing against her magic. Was this the *thing* that the Cysgod had warned them about?

At that moment Durand spun around her and sliced her side. The pain and blood shocked her, and the failing magic of her sword filled her fragile heart with fear. She felt a shadow pass over her life as they both paused, eyes locked from only a few feet away.

He smiled wickedly. "Your magic falters, witch. Jhoras shields his anointed—you are nothing!"

Isolde lifted her Cynddaredd purposefully in front of her, trying to make her motion of defiance banish her fear and doubt. "I will still kill you, mongrel dog."

His eyes lit with the cold fury of madness. During the last frantic chaos of strikes, Isolde felt the thorned thing pushing against her magic again, trying to sever it from her.

They paused, eyeing one another, new wounds bleeding. She stepped back away from him carefully, over one of the corpses she had left earlier, and smiled with satisfaction. There was a deep bloody gash along the Inquisitor's collarbone, and his pretty white robes were now drenched in red. "How can you be so callous with destruction? Even your own men were fed to that insanity."

His mouth cracked into that same wicked grin, blood dripping down his face and robes. "The Will of Jhoras shines brightly upon the anointed. Though some glow in that light, others must feed the flames as it spreads. Every anointed knows the cost of their faith." He took a slow measured step toward her, his grin widening. "Your magic is strong. I needed you to use it first—to tire!"

Their blades met again as he lunged forward. He was right, she was tiring. She could feel it as she blocked him and retreated again. She was wounded, cuts bleeding all over her bruised and beaten body. Worse, without the lightning of Cynddaredd's magic this was a normal fight and he, being a man, had the edge. But Isolde felt her sword trying to break free—she had to think.

As they separated, both panting, more Aedonian forces entered the large throne room. She watched them cautiously while holding Cynddaredd in front of herself.

The men parted, making a pathway, while drawing blades and raising shields protectively. She heard him first; his heavy footfalls echoed like thunder against her heart. Then he was there, Gregoire D'Arganse, High King of Aedonia.

Isolde blinked the blood from her eyes and took another step backwards, trying to banish her fear. She tried to focus beyond her pain, exhaustion, and sadness. It was then that Isolde sensed the object itself. A relic made of thorns, like the Cysgod had warned them of, somehow pulsing with the pain of her wounds, trying to take her magic away. Isolde was sure this was the thing stealing their magic from her sisters. Whatever it was this Inquisitor had, Isolde felt Cynddaredd pushing against it earlier. She could break it, freeing her sisters. If she could kill him, and the bastard Aedonian king in the process, all the better. It would be a final act, her sacrifice to save those of her sisters that still lived.

As if fate itself, or Rhiannon, had heard her, Gregoire stepped forward to join Inquisitor Durand. The king smiled. "Queen Isolde, it is good to see you again." He looked around the room noting the corpses, the debris, and the flames with seeming disgust. "Though I must say it was under nicer circumstances last time." He paused for a moment as if remembering, drawing out the grim juxtaposition between his calm words and the carnage that surrounded them. "The Daphshire Grand Ball, wasn't it?" He saw the resolve, the anger, and the grief in her eyes as she lifted Cynddaredd higher. "You have fought so hard, and I tire of this slaughter. Surrender now and your death will be painless, I give you my word." More men flooded into the room, surrounding her, the king, and the Inquisitor.

She raised Cynddaredd higher and turned the blade downwards. Her sword had one more final power, one that would kill them all and destroy everything around her. "Your word means nothing to me, traitorous charlatan." The words came easier than she had expected. It was an ending to this life and the beginning of her journey into Byd Nesaf. Isolde silently prayed to Rhiannon for her husband Cormac, her son Cian, and those of her sisters, then she spoke. "Dydd Dial a Marwolaeth yn dod." She shoved Cynddaredd into the floor, a last act of pure will that would shatter both her and the sword, releasing what remained of their magic. "Brenhines yn sefyll!" The day of vengeance and death is coming. A queen stands!

Cynddaredd's lightning came again, one last time, arcing around her in a wild pulsing circle, igniting the very air with flame. Stray bolts shot out everywhere, hitting shields, swords, and soldiers with magical fury, seeking to destroy. Breaking and igniting everything they touched into flames. Isolde felt the thorns break, felt her magic flow back to full strength, and in those heartbeats the real explosion began, shaking the large throne room and seeking to consume everything in its path.

Inquisitor Durand leapt forward toward High King Gregoire, holding the three-quartered Jhorian cross around his neck, as a halo of pale light appeared around the two men. A shield. "Majesty!"

Her enemies would live, but her sisters were free now. Isolde's life force winked out as her body was consumed in flames and the large throne room started collapsing into piles of fiery debris; the entire castle shook with the resounding boom of her heart's last moments.

．　．　．　．　．　．

Cormac shoved the drawbar into place and put the palm of his hand on the castle's stone wall for a brief moment in silent prayer, desperately trying to catch his breath. A faint tremor shook the stone, as if Isolde's fury stirred above. Cormac wished his beautiful Isolde was with him, but she was still out there, having chosen to stay behind and delay their enemy, even with the castle burning and their people dying. Some might have called it foolish pride, or even a failure on his part as a man, but he knew her. She was powerful, resolute, and had the heart of the knight and queen that she was. Arguing with her was like screaming at a mountain to move from your path. Cormac also had his duty to save their son Cian, and he would not fail.

Cormac turned around and started striding down the long hallway. It was quieter here for now, but the walls were cracked, and he could hear the distant sounds of battle. Then the sounds came closer as he heard them outside the door he'd just barred, banging and calling for a battering ram.

Cormac didn't have long, and there were only a few men still with him, but they were Cathyoran. These few would be enough.

He looked at them. "Owain, Dylan, stay here and slow them down as much as you can. May Rhiannon have mercy on your souls and guide you into the next world." He kissed his fingers and touched each man's chest.

"Yes, Majesty!" They drew their blades and turned back toward the far door. Both paused for a moment, nodding respectfully to another of the men with them, who returned the silent gesture.

Cormac swept onward, followed by the remaining few of his men. They all knew their duty and loved Cian as their own. Cormac looked at the man next to him. He didn't know the man, but the men treated him with respect and there was a sergeant's mark on his breastplate. "What's your name, soldier?" Normally he would know every man near him and his family, but today had been full of chaos and death; it was impossible for a king to know every man in his service, especially in times like these.

The man nodded stolidly, matching his pace. "Sergeant Archibald Stallwood, Your Majesty."

He nodded in return, recognizing the man's calm. Even in crisis a good soldier was owed his due. "Good man. Have they found Brianna?"

Archibald glanced back briefly as a new round of pounding began on the doorway. "Yes, Majesty, she is in the royal nursery with prince Cian."

"Thank Rhiannon. Has there been any word from the Trefn Cyfiawnder coming back from their mission?" He knew those in the city were overwhelmed. Somehow the Aedonians had disabled much of their order's magic.

Archibald's eyes grew saddened. "No word, Your Majesty. They must have been ambushed."

"How convenient. What about those still in the city or Gwarchodlu Brenhinol?" He already knew the answer. He'd sent most of his royal guard to help evacuate civilians and every woman of Trefn Cyfiawnder, but it was good to keep his men talking and thinking.

His new companion sighed, obviously tired and distraught. "They are bogged down by invading Aedonians last I heard, Majesty. Almost as though they were targeted, and their magic isn't working."

"Damn them all." Cormac turned down the short hallway toward his son's nursery and the small throne room, with its escape passage.

They finally arrived outside and Brianna was indeed already there. He smiled, offering a silent prayer to Rhiannon.

Entering the room, Cormac looked down at Cian, the last Ahearne. He touched his son's cheek and allowed a tear to fall. Brianna looked at him, eyes full of love and sorrow.

"Brianna. You must take Cian and Dygwr Tynged to safety."

Tears welled up in her eyes. "Majesty..."

He put his hand on the side of her face. "Please, Brianna. They're going to break through. Our family, my son must survive—nothing else matters now."

Cormac almost nodded at his own words, because they were true. His kingdom was gone. His son had to live. He put a hand on her shoulder, squeezing gently. "The small throne room's escape passage should still be intact. Do this last thing for your king."

Brianna's eyes, weathered by generations, held firm; she knew her duty. Cormac gently strapped Dygwr Tynged or "Fatebringer," the House Ahearne sword, around her back. Then picked up his son and kissed him one last time before handing him to her. "May Rhiannon have mercy on your soul old friend. Be well and thank you."

He kissed his fingers and touched her chest. She nodded, still crying, and fled down the hallway toward the small throne room, with Carwyn and another soldier named Gethin as escorts. Carrying his son, the Ahearne family legacy, and Cathyor's last hope to safety, Cormac watched her go for a brief moment, fondly remembering a lifetime of care and love. In Brianna's arms, his son would be safe.

Cormac stepped back into the hallway and looked toward the far doorway on his way to join the men he'd left there, with Archibald in tow. His beautiful Isolde was making her final stand and had entrusted him with the life of their son. She had always believed in him, and now it was time to show her that he was worthy of her love and trust. His people called him king, but it had always been her he needed to live up to. It might be his final moments, but Cormac would be the man worthy of a woman like Isolde until his last breath.

Suddenly the whole castle shook violently with a resounding boom from above. He and Archibald locked arms and used the corridor walls to stay standing. Afterwards, Cormac closed his eyes for a moment, a deep feeling of loss settling into his heart. He silently said a prayer to Rhiannon for his beautiful Isolde's soul, his son, and the kingdom.

The faraway doorway broke open and Aedonian soldiers flooded in, engaging Owain and Dylan, as rubble fell from the ceiling and flames seemed found their way into the corridor from nowhere.

Cormac pulled a sword off the nearby weapons rack; it wasn't Dygwr Tynged, but it would have to do. He and Archibald met one another's gazes and nodded before facing their enemies. It was time to look fate in the eyes.

CHAPTER TWO:
BYWYD A MARWOLAETH
(LIFE AND DEATH)

The castle shook again, as if dying with him. Cormac pulled his sword from the Aedonian man's chest, his breath ragged. The corpse fell among rubble, blood pooling on white tiles.

They heard more soldiers coming from the other corridor. They tiredly crossed blades and readied themselves. The day had been a long one and it wasn't over yet.

"Byw yw marw." Archibald spoke the words in a voice raspy with exhaustion. He too understood their meaning, and what was coming. "Marw yw byw."

Archibald was a good soldier. They'd only met recently but the man was Cathyoran to the core, and it was good to have another of his people with him. They were going to die, but the men of Cathyor knew how to face such things: With a blade in their hands, the words on their lips, and their hearts dedicated to each other.

There were more soldiers this time, and he glimpsed crossbowmen behind them too. There was a certain elegance to waging war inside of corridors and wearing an opponent down. Once trapped, the enemy had little choice but to play a game of defense and withdrawal. If this were better times, and he was a lesser man, being caught in that trap would hurt his pride. Gregoire D'Arganse, the Aedonian King, was many things, but a fool was not one of them.

With a brief look at his companion and a nod, they both carefully withdrew past another crossing corridor, tiredly stepping over rubble and around flaming debris to take cover behind two pillars as quickly as they could. Several heartbeats later the enemy hit them like a screaming river of violence. Shields slammed forward. Blades clashed. The violent flow abated to a trickle, however, as the pillars he and Archibald were sheltering behind started functioning as a choke point. It would protect them from the crossbowmen if they were careful. Their enemy wasn't foolish, but neither was he. Cormac had been in many battles throughout his life and was known as a highly capable war leader himself. If he was going to die today, so would as many of the enemy as he could manage.

As the enemy soldiers hit, he and Archibald went to work. They traded targets—swinging, blocking, and thrusting while the other took cover, sometimes moving in perfect unison. The choke point quickly turned into a storm of clashing steel and blood. Battle was always hot, bloody chaos, and this one was no exception. Cormac could feel the blood pounding through his veins with every movement, slicking his grip, draining his strength, staining his skin red. Another enemy soldier came into view with sword and shield, going for his side, but in so doing the man had to turn his back to Archibald, which was his final mistake.

The next one went for Archibald's underarm as he withdrew. They were both slower from the long day of fighting, but Cormac was ready for it, tired as he was. His blade sank deep into the enemy soldier's stomach, eliciting a scream and a river of blood as he pulled it back out. But then the rhythm of battle was interrupted as a shock of pain ripped through Cormac's right arm, nearly making him drop his sword.

He staggered behind the pillar and leaned against the wall, gasping for breath, pain and exhaustion consuming him. For a moment he considered pulling the crossbow bolt out, but there was no time—and doing so might make him bleed more, losing what little strength he had left. At least it struck his right arm and not his left sword arm. He looked at Archibald, who, though not as grievously wounded, still looked completely spent. "It's time, brother."

Archibald nodded, as the castle shook again, as if it also understood. They were both tired, injured, and outnumbered; it was time to make their last stand.

Archibald's voice was strained and tired, but he was Cathyoran. "I stand with you, brother. A last charge—for Cathyor and love!"

Just before they sprang into the open corridor, a distant clash echoed down the hall, then a woman's voice screamed from behind their enemy's line. "Majesty! Hold fast—I'm here!"

The enemy soldiers lost a step, between engaging Cormac and Archibald and the new sounds of battle now coming from behind them.

Flashing arcs of blinding white light and screams started coming from the end of the corridor. "Crogwyr's magic still works! Come, bastards, feel my wrath!"

A smile spread across Archibald's face as they charged in, hitting the confused enemy soldiers hard. "Elspeth?!"

"Archibald! My love! How? Thank Rhiannon!"

Cormac smiled as he blocked another blow and Archibald struck the man down. He knew Elspeth, one of his most loyal Gwarchodlu Brenhinol, who had been with him for years now. She had apparently chosen to disobey his orders and stay behind. It was good, even in these times of chaos and death, his people's love still survived.

The sounds of battle intensified, and then they could see her between enemy movements. Elspeth Anwyl was a champion swordswoman, and she was living up to the title. Flashes of her sword's white magic and the blood of their enemies streaked through air around her as she swept through them. Cormac would have laughed, had it been happier times. There were two dead knights—and not just common soldiers—lying on the blood-stained tile floor behind her; it was always a marvel watching a woman of Trefn Cyfiawnder in battle.

When the last emeny soldier fell, they came together and Cormac's two companions embraced each other fiercely. Cormac smiled. He'd never gotten the chance to meet Elspeth's love before, but now apparently, he had, and he was indeed a good man.

"Archibald, I thought I'd lost you. My heart is alive—praise Rhiannon!"

After a few fervent moments of kissing, Archibald stepped back.

His voice was still raspy, but it sounded lighter too. "I found my way to his Majesty during the turmoil, because I was looking for you." Archibald looked at Cormac, a bit embarrassed. "I'm sorry, Majesty, a soldier should know his duty."

Cormac laughed and painfully pushed himself from the wall he'd been leaning against and onto his feet. He'd leaned there, resting his arm during their reunion. "Never apologize for love, you are Cathyoran." He looked down the corridor Elspeth had come from; there were more enemy footsteps headed in their direction.

Elspeth stepped in front of him and nodded. "You are hurt, Majesty. Stay behind me. I will protect you both."

Cormac smiled sadly. The women of their order were so loyal and had such strong hearts. "No. My dear Isolde already gave her life to release your magic and slow them down. I will do the same, something of our people's love will survive this day."

Her eyes became sad. "That's why I can feel Calon again, and Crogwyr lives? My sister." She shook herself and turned toward the enemy still far off. "I will stop them. The two of you, go."

Cormac put a hand on her shoulder. "No. Obey your king this one last time. Take Archibald with you and retreat. I will stand here. Love will survive."

They both looked shocked and answered almost simultaneously. "Majesty, no. I will not leave you."

"I forbid it! I am your king and this my choice. The love of my people must survive, even if it's only the two of you and my son. Find prince Cian if you can and protect him—now go!" They did not move. "Now! Use the small throne room's escape passage and flee. That is your king's final request—obey me and live, love." He kissed his fingers and touched each of their chests as they both finally nodded.

Elspeth spoke first. "I promise you I will find and protect the prince. Your son will endure, I swear it."

Then Archibald spoke. "Byw yw marw."

"Marw yw byw." They left him and Cormac smiled as he turned to wait for the enemy. Cathyor had fallen and his beloved Isolde was gone. But Cian and his people would live, and with them the Cathyoran heart.

The first of his new enemy appeared at the end of the corridor. He charged, ignoring his heartache and pain, as the castle shook again and the flames intensified. "Dydd Dial a Marwolaeth yn dod!" The day of vengeance and death is coming!

· · · · · ·

Marged woke gasping, pinned under her sisters' corpses, pain seared her body.

Finally—after how long she didn't know—she felt strong enough to move. Marged took a deep breath and heaved again and again. Eventually the pile on top of her shifted with a sickening sound, and she could see the sky. Marged turned her head, and through her blood-matted red hair, she was greeted by a dead face, one that she knew. Her sister Rhys's skull was caved in. Terror gripped her and Marged screamed, until her voice went hoarse and she was trembling in shock.

Eventually Marged calmed and remembered. They had been ambushed by the combined force of Aedonians and Jhorians. Their magic had failed them. Marged remembered the moment Aerona's presence had vanished, and her blades faltered. She shuddered at remembering that terror and feeling the weight of her dead sisters on top of her. She was the only survivor.

Ailbhe's fate flashed through her mind, a year-old wound. Had the same thing happened to her back then? Did their enemies have a new weapon capable of defeating their magic? Had her sister's death been a warning?

Marged gasped, her eyes widening with new horror. She had to warn Brynn! They would be going after the king and his family.

Purpose filled her and she pulled herself out of the pile. Struggling for breath, Marged rolled out from under the bodies of her sisters and onto her hands and knees.

She gazed at them. So many of her sisters were gone. Marged started weeping and retching onto the ground in a complete loss of awareness.

Whatever had been left in her stomach was gone now. Marged closed her eyes, and time slipped away until she was finally able to leverage herself up and stand, if unsteadily.

She found her misericordias, Poen and Rheolaeth or "Pain and Death," and sheathed them. A torn Trefn Cyfiawnder cloak, marked by its sacred tree and sword, lay at her feet; she threw it over her shoulders. Who had it belonged to? Which of her dead sisters' cloak was she wearing?

Grief welled up again and Marged closed her eyes, letting it stream down her cheeks and into the dirt at her feet.

Marged opened her eyes and turned to look down the long roadway toward Brynn, their beloved capital, only to see her home in flames. The distant smoke and fire rose skyward, taking her hopes away.

She fell to her knees and started shaking. There weren't enough tears left for this, not anymore. Her eyes closed again, unable to witness so much death and loss any longer. Utter despair engulfed her as the world went black.

Marged's sleep was filled with nightmares. She had no magic, because her Dryad was gone. Aerona was dead. Brynn, the capital of her beloved home, was burning. Charnel piles of her sisters' corpses seemed to fade into the sky, turning it black with terror and sadness. But then she felt something, a flickering presence, a powerful magic that she knew. Aerona was not dead. Marged could feel her, weaker and intermittent, but she was still there. Alive.

The sound of loud creaking tree branches woke her, as if they were caught in a ferocious wind. Marged opened her eyes and found she could still cry. Tears streamed down her face as she looked up toward the nearby forest and saw the Dryads.

The giant feminine titans looked like they were half tree and half beautiful goddess. Though they lived in the next world, each was bonded to a woman of Trefn Cyfiawnder. This was where their order's magical power and swords came from.

Their beautiful eyes gazed upon her from above the distant tree line, exuding peace, compassion, love, and understanding. Their magic—her sisters' swords—had broken today yet now stirred again. The Dryads started moving forward, each of them would carry one of her dead sisters into Byd Nesaf, ushering their beloved souls on the next part of their journey.

Aerona stopped in front of Marged and looked down sadly. Tears started falling down her face and splashing the ground in front of her as Marged looked up and screamed, her voice hoarse with grief. "I'm sorry I failed you..."

The words caught in Marged's throat as Aerona, her Dryad, knelt down and embraced her gently. Those giant eyes met her own as the Dryad's voice engulfed Marged like a warm summer breeze. "Llefain fy mhlentyn, y mae hwn yn ddydd o dristwch i ni oll, ond nid eiddot ti yr euogrwydd i'w gadw. Gadewch iddo fynd." Cry my child, this is a day of sorrow for us all, but the guilt is not yours to keep. Let it go.

Marged laid her head in Aerona's hands and wept, as the other Dryads stood and walked past them back toward the trees, carrying her sisters away. She knew their swords would vanish now, in a last glimpse of their power, signaling the transition of their souls into Byd Nesaf.

Eventually, Aerona gently picked Marged up, cradling her as she cried, and carried her away into the forest.

CHAPTER THREE:
GRYM YR ABERTH
(THE POWER OF SACRIFICE)

Brianna ran, desperation fueling her strength despite her burning lungs, until her legs faltered, forcing her against a stone wall to catch her breath. It was raining and the cobblestones were wet. She had felt her feet threaten to slip more than once, but she couldn't stop or slow down. They would kill her and baby prince Cian if she stopped for too long.

Lightning and thunder broke the sky above, making her flinch. She could almost feel the shock and horror in the tremulous beating of her heart. The day had been full of violence and death, now highlighted by the fires burning all across their beloved city of Brynn. Even the heavy rain couldn't douse those flames, as if their people's doom was a prophecy.

A few terror-filled heartbeats later, she prayed to Rhiannon and pushed herself up. Her escort of soldiers was gone; they'd stayed back to fight off their pursuit a few streets ago. She had no idea where it was safe or how many Aedonian soldiers were still following her.

Her back screamed in pain from the combined weight of Prince Cian and the House Ahearne sword. Brianna had never imagined that her service as House Ahearne's biume would end this way. She was supposed to be enjoying her pension on the servants' estate, not fleeing for her life with the new baby prince. But she loved the Ahearnes like family. She might be exhausted and facing death, but Brianna would not fail them.

Brianna hugged Prince Cian against her chest tightly as she heard horse hooves in the distance, coming toward them. She darted toward another street but stopped, seeing Aedonian soldiers there too.

Brianna stumbled, her lungs burning and heart pounding with desperation. What was she going to do? If they caught her tonight all of Cathyor would fall, forever. Because they would kill Prince Cian. Fresh tears started falling down her cheeks, as she quietly prayed for deliverance, or at least mercy.

The horses she'd heard were closer now. Their hooves sounded like thunder and doom to her ears. "Rhiannon, please...?"

Then, with squealing loud enough to wake the dead let alone startle her already fragile nerves, the door to a candlemaker's shop opened to her left. A kindly looking middle-aged man stuck his head out and looked at her.

"My lady? I am Tomas, please follow me. We will get you out."

Brianna hesitated. How could she trust this unknown man? He looked kind but a person's eyes were easy to deceive. Then she saw the Aedonian cavalry coming closer. She followed the man into the shop. What other choice did she have? There was nowhere else to go. He moved aside, letting her enter the small shop while he looked down the street both ways and quickly closed the door behind them. Her voice trembled, weak in her own ears. "Thank you. I don't know what we would have done without you."

He smiled before heading toward the opposite wall.

"You are both very welcome, my lady, please come with me." He motioned for her to hurry. "Quickly."

Brianna stopped in shock as a shelf against the wall moved to reveal a tunnel and a small child, who looked maybe ten with blond hair and startling blue eyes, holding a lantern. The child's eyes were reddened, and her cheeks were tear-stained, but they focused immediately, noting the House Ahearne sword on Brianna's back, lingering on its hilt and then moving to Prince Cian.

"Thank Rhiannon we found them in time."

Tomas bowed to her. "Yes, my lady. She and young Prince Cian are both well."

The girl touched a hand to her heart. "Thank Rhiannon." She turned away to walk down the tunnel. "Come with me. Tomas will close the tunnel behind you."

Brianna looked at the little blonde girl. "But... you're a child!"

The girl stopped, laughing with a touch of rueful sadness. "I didn't get much choice, unfortunately. They ambushed my mother, and the other women of Trefn Cyfiawnder, they're all gone..." The girl choked. "We are all that's left." She met Brianna's eyes defiantly. "I'll die before they take the prince!"

Brianna tried to hide her shock at the girl's fervor and followed her as Tomas closed the tunnel's entrance behind them. "Who are you?"

The girl looked back. "You may call me Morrigan."

A sharp intake of breath came from Tomas behind her. "My lady..."

Morrigan laughed again. "Hush, Tomas. Who would she tell—the Aedonians?" She looked at Brianna. "I am Morrigan Bresling, daughter of Meabh Bresling."

Brianna missed a step, recovering herself quickly. The Bresling family was one of the oldest and most powerful of Trefn Cyfiawnder bloodlines.

Morrigan nodded. "You know who I am. Good." She took a step toward them and gently laid a hand on Prince Cian. "Has he been marked with the House Ahearne sigil yet?"

"Uh yes... He has been marked."

The girl sighed. "That is well, our prince should bear his family's mark, but it makes our path harder." She sighed, looking tired and sad, like they all did. "Tomas, we will have to use the supply wagons. There's no other way to get them past the soldiers. They'll be looking for a marked baby boy." Morrigan turned away again and started walking down the darkened tunnel. "Come along you two, we have a long night ahead of us."

Brianna followed the girl's lantern into the tunnel, thinking it was like a beacon in the dark, a last hope for them all.

· · · · · ·

Cormac knelt in the castle's ruins. He knew it was finally over; he could feel it deep down in his soul. Even the castle knew and was now settling down into quiet dullness after the war waged within its walls. He wondered, as he kneeled and looked out the nearby windows, past the enemy, if this was what his dear Isolde had felt in her final moments. It was nearing evening and it was raining heavily, as if Innatraea herself was also mourning the loss of Cathyor.

Cormac's entire body hurt. He'd lost count of the wounds he suffered throughout the day, not to mention the huge gash on his right arm that was still leaking blood. Even his knees hurt from kneeling, waiting for it to be over. He silently prayed to Rhiannon for his soul to rest soon.

At least Archibald and Elspeth had listened to him and fled. His people's love would survive this day. Somewhere inside he found the will to smile, one last piece of joy in this life.

Gregoire D'Arganse, the Aedonian High King and his enemy, glared from his place standing above Cormac. "Your kingdom burns, your wife is dead, your people with her, and you smile?!"

Cormac laughed while gasping in pain, almost choking on his own blood. "You don't yet understand what you have done. Aedonia is doomed." He coughed up more blood. "The people of Cathyor are rooted deep in this world, we are the seeds Innatraea's Great Trees. You cannot kill us so easily."

Gregoire slapped him with his gauntleted fist, sending Cormac onto his hands and knees. "I don't understand?! Cathyor and its people are done! You will die here today!"

Cormac gasped in pain, coughing up blood. "Dydd Dial a Marwolaeth yn dod!" The day of vengeance and death is coming!

Gregoire pulled Cormac's head back by his hair and looked into his eyes. "She died chanting that, yet I stand!"

Her face appeared in his thoughts, his dear beautiful beloved Isolde. Soon their souls would be together again in Byd Nesaf. If he were a lesser man and still had a life left to live, these final moments might cause despair and shame in his heart. But Gregoire didn't know everything. Isolde had released their magic, Trefn Cyfiawnder would survive, his people and their love would live on, and most importantly his son, Cian, would grow up. None of them had been defeated on even ground, the numerous crossbow bolts riddling his body spoke to that. Cormac closed his eyes and remained quiet, anger and hatred would do no good here; it was best to remain quiet and die in his own way. It would be nice to see Isolde again. She was waiting for him beyond all this pain.

"You still smile at a time like this?! Your mad ilk stains Innatraea. Good riddance!"

Gregoire's blade flashed, and the world disappeared, as Cormac's pain ended.

. . . . . .

Aisling's foot slipped on the wet cobblestones and her knee hit the ground so hard that tears welled in her eyes. She held onto the babies though and didn't cry out. They were so little, not understanding silence or its urgency, so both baby girls cried again. She didn't blame them. In truth, Aisling wanted to cry too. Everything in their world had changed in an instant, becoming so terrible she couldn't think about it without wanting to weep. But right now, lives depended on her. Briallen and Eira Bishop were just babies, their mother Ceridwen had died earlier that day while helping them all escape. Aisling blinked her eyes clear of tears and looked down the street at her own mother.

"Rydw i wedi dod yn farwolaeth!" her mother screamed while hitting an Aedonian soldier in the face with her shield and swinging her sword to slice another down his side. Aisling knew the old tongue, like all of them did. The words meant that her mother had become death itself—maybe they all had by now. Her mother's cloak blew in the wind, the tree and sword sewn into rippled with the wind's fury. As it flew, her body disappeared behind its magic, reappearing when the wind blew a different direction. She moved through the soldiers gracefully, the fiery magic of her sword cutting off limbs and stabbing sides, burning her enemies as she evaded blows. She had always taught Aisling to keep her word, and so tonight she was going to, becoming a flaming vengeful death for the men who sought to annihilate them.

Her mother didn't look back, but her voice crossed the distance between them, cutting into Aisling's heart like lightning. "Aisling! My love, you have to go. Find Morrigan! Now run!" A crossbow bolt hit her mother's shield hard and more soldiers came from another street, charging them. Her mother screamed, blocking another incoming bolt as she fell to one knee.

Her mother was right. She had a promise to keep now also. After tonight none of them were really children any longer, and she had given her word. She and the babies had to survive. "Fe wnaf o fam, dwi'n addo!" I'll do it, Mother, I promise!

Aisling pushed herself to her feet, still holding the crying babies close. Then she turned and ran, tears streaming down her face, with the fiery steel of her mother's sword and screams of their enemy echoing behind her. It started raining again.

Chapter Four:
Tân Torcalon
(The Fire of Heartbreak)

Morrigan stared out the carriage window into the dark, rain-soaked night, past burning houses and strewn corpses, her grief mirroring Cathyor's ruin

What was she supposed to feel? The sadness and loss were almost too powerful for her to bear, but she had no choice—there was no one else.

The rain fell harder, and too late to save a city already in ashes. Something moved in the distance, coming toward them, a small form running through the rain. She couldn't see much through the smoky haze that hung over the city in the early evening dimness.

The small form became clearer as it neared them, emerging from the darkness in a rush, and Morrigan gasped, yelling at the driver. "HALT!" The carriage ground to a stop and Morrigan jumped out into the rain, as the small form came running straight toward her. "Thank Rhiannon. Aisling!"

Morrigan embraced her friend around the babies she was carrying, then took one of them from her. "Tomas, come help us with the babies, please."

He was already there, gently taking the babies from them before getting back into the carriage. "Of course, My Lady."

Morrigan looked at her friend. "You're alright. I'm so glad. Your mother? Are these the Bishop twins?" Aisling sobbed and Morrigan hugged her tighter. "I'm sorry."

Aisling hugged her back fiercely. "I was so afraid." She started crying harder. "I thought we were alone... They're the Bishop twins."

"We're together now. We can make it through this."

"We'll make it, together."

Morrigan hugged her again. "Get into the carriage. We have to get everyone somewhere safe."

Morrigan was still climbing into the carriage when her shouts echoed down the street. Aedonian soldiers—they must have been chasing Aisling.

She was tired and sad—heartbroken—they all were. But a flash of anger ignited deep within her. She had felt their magic come back earlier, though she still didn't understand how the Aedonians had sealed it in the first place. But whatever had broken it freed them.

Damn whoever had helped them do that. Had it not happened, they'd never have caught us defenseless. That had changed now, she could feel it, and though only a few of her people still lived, they were a dangerous few. It was time the enemy felt their pain. Morrigan stepped out into the road, ignoring shouts from the carriage, and drew the knife from her belt.

Lightning and thunder crashed as it started raining harder, and the soldiers came into view. Morrigan dragged the knife along her forearm, chanting as her blood fell onto the ground. "Duwies Rhiannon. Rwy'n galw tân. Rwy'n galw marwolaeth." Goddess Rhiannon. I call fire. I call death.

Pain seared her arm as her blood hit the ground, summoning her mother's blade—Gwr gweddw, or "Widowmaker"—appeared before her, hovering in the air. The blade glinted blue as lightning flashed before settling into her outstretched hand. It was heavy, and her arm was screaming in pain from the cut she'd made. Her vision swam, but she tensed her core and focused on the power of her magic—just like her mother had taught her. Two of the nearby buildings went up in flames on either side of the Aedonian soldiers, collapsing before flooding the street in flaming debris and death.

Morrigan almost buckled from the pain in her arm, but Tomas was there to catch her and helped her into the carriage before wrapping a cloth around her forearm. "Pace yourself, My Lady—today's a nightmare."

She smiled at him tiredly and nodded. "Thank you, Tomas." She looked out the carriage window as it started moving, remembering her mother and feeling that deep pang of loss anew. She heard Meabh's voice: "Mae pŵer a phoen yr un peth yn aml." Power and pain are often the same thing.

Archibald pushed the passageway door open and looked out into the darkening evening. It was raining, there were still fires everywhere, and the sounds of shouting or fighting came from every direction, but there was no one in sight in their immediate vicinity. He turned back and gently put his hand on Elspeth's shoulder. She was looking back at the way they'd come, her eyes filled with grief and indecision. The King had told them to go, and they'd obeyed, but she had been Gwarchodlu Brenhinol; it had been her duty to protect Cathyor's Royal family.

"My love? We need to go. The street is clear, but it won't stay that way for long, the city has descended into chaos." She looked at him, tears in her eyes. "He told us to go. Our duty now is to live."

She finally nodded, and let him pull her out into the dark night. "We need to help whoever we can, Archibald, my sister and her daughter…"

"We'll help all we can as we flee, I swear. We're close to the Bishop Estate, where your sister was. We'll check there, but staying here any longer is certain death."

She squeezed his hand and nodded, though her voice was still heavy with emotion. "My heart, thank you."

Moving through the streets was a harrowing affair. They needed to avoid Aedonian patrols, mobs, and the fires that seemed to be everywhere. Archibald looked at Elspeth, while they huddled in an alleyway, waiting for a large enemy group to pass. She looked at him from under the cloak he'd found for her, the dead soldier he'd taken it off no longer needed it. Her eyes were raw with emotion but there was also anger, resolve, love, and trust in that gaze. She must be experiencing so much. He couldn't imagine the pain that must be residing in her heart; his own seemed small at the thought of it. Once again, he found himself praying to Rhiannon that this would not be where she chose to release those feelings with her blade. Elspeth was strong, but she was tired and heartbroken. Plus, they were severely outnumbered and most of the enemy groups they'd seen included knights and Inquisitors.

The large group of enemies finally passed and slowly disappeared around another corner. Once their boots faded, Archibald and Elspeth moved again, trying to be cautious, though they wanted to cover as much ground as possible before they had to hide again. A few streets later they were stood in front of the Bishop Estate, which was engulfed in flames. Elspeth let go of Archibald's hand and stepped forward, as if she was going to run into the flames, but he grabbed her arm to stop her and she looked back at him, fear-stricken and angry. "We have to go in there and see if anyone survived. Archibald, we have to!"

He sighed and tried to speak gently even though all he felt was rage and despair. "We can't do that, my love, anyone still in there is gone, the entire estate is in flames. Going inside now would only bring our own deaths as well." As he spoke, Archibald watched her face transition from anger, to disbelief, and finally to the sadness of acceptance.

"We have to go now, nowhere in Brynn is safe," he continued. She merely nodded and silently let him pull her away, which was worse than if she'd fought. He didn't look back at her, for fear of what he'd see in her eyes, and instead just kept them moving toward the city's edge and eventual safety.

As they were passed another side street, she let go of his hand before screaming and running away from him. "Brighid!"

Archibald followed her without hesitation or argument—the name she had screamed was her sister's. She ran and collapsed next to Brighid, who was sitting on the ground, leaning against the flaming wall of a small house. She was covered in wounds and blood. Elspeth wrapped her arms protectively around her, heedless of her sister's wounds and blood, hugging her close. "Brighid, my sister."

Brighid slowly moved to look at Elspeth, her eyes coming into focus, and she coughed blood. "Sister? My Aisling, I think she escaped, she had the babies..."

Elspeth put her forehead against her sister's. "Our magic is back. I will find her, I promise you. She has the Bishop twins with her?"

Brighid spasmed in pain and choked, spitting up more blood, before answering. Her voice sounded raspy and got quieter as she spoke. "Yes." Her hand slowly lifted and touched Elspeth's face. "I'm dying, little sister. Find the children. Protect my little Aisling." As if she had spoken her final wish, Brighid's head slowly rolled forward and her hand fell limply to the ground.

Elspeth put a hand on Brighid's face, gently closing her sister's eyes and hugging her close as she wept. "Gorffwyswch nawr, fy chwaer. Boed i chi ddod o hyd i heddwch yn y Byd Nesaf." Rest now, my sister. May you find peace in the next world. Elspeth kissed Brighid's hair gently. "I will find them."

Elspeth started carefully wrapping Brighid in the cloak Archibald had found earlier, a burial much less honorable than she deserved, but he would help Elspeth carry her sister into the forest. Safety or not, it was a matter of honor and respect every man owed the women of Trefn Cyfiawnder. They were different from other Cathyorans, who burned their dead to usher their loved ones' journeys into Byd Nesaf. The women of Trefn Cyfiawnder were buried in the forest, amongst the trees, their sacred haven. Elspeth reverently placed her hand on the hilt of Brighid's sword, quietly closing her eyes

Then, out of nowhere, shouting echoed down the street. "Another of the godless witches! Kill her!"

Archibald felt something in the air change, and a pressure seemed to emanate from Elspeth. He drew his sword and looked over at her.

Her eyes opened and she choked, gasping. Then her whole body tensed, as she gulped back her tears. Elspeth stood slowly, gathering herself, and then she looked at him.

In her eyes he saw an unimaginable amount of pure rage. She had chosen her moment and all he could do was accompany her in what was to come.

A dozen foes were almost amongst them, including knights and an Inquisitor. But Elspeth didn't hurry, she merely drew her sword and reached out with her other arm. Archibald could almost hear the dirge of doom visible in Elspeth's eyes as her sister's sword flew to her outstretched hand. Both blades glowed, one pure white and the other flaming red, as she silently stepped into the street to meet their enemies. Archibald stood frozen in fear and awe, watching, unable to move. It was as if Brighid's spirit fueled her now.

Lightning cracked through the sky, followed by the resounding boom of thunder, as she met the enemy charge. There was nothing they could do to stop her. Elspeth's rage had become a storm of magic and steel, freezing, burning, maiming, and piercing them at every turn, sending blood, icy pieces, and flaming chunks of her enemies flying into the night air. By the time it was over, only moments later, she had started wordlessly screaming, and the few survivors left fled in terror. Even the Inquisitor tried to flee, but it ended with him on the ground, both swords shoved through his chest, pulsing their magic into his lifeless corpse until it shattered into pieces at her feet.

Elspeth stood there, weeping and screaming, as if waiting for either more foes to come or the heartache she felt to take her away. Archibald sheathed his sword and slowly walked up to her, carefully avoiding pieces of the now dead Aedonians. He gently laid a hand on Elspeth's shoulder. Her breath rasped and her arms trembled as she lowered both swords.

"My love?"

Elspeth looked at him silently, her eyes somewhere else, as if she was trying to find something she couldn't see. It started raining again. Elspeth shook herself, and though there was still grief and loss there, her eyes focused, meeting his own. "We can't leave yet—we must find the Bishop twins, my niece, and the prince."

Chapter Five: House Dupris

The carriage halted on a quieter street, chaos raging beyond. Hours delayed, Morrigan dreaded the lives lost, yet Banque Dupris's guards recognized her, Lady Morrigan Bresling, and would let them inside. This was one of their last gambits, a secret that would keep them safe and allow their plans for the future. She hated to use it, had hoped that they'd never have to, and now here they were, leveraging their mother's last contingency.

Morrigan looked up at the faces of those with her. Tomas held the Bishop twins, who were sleeping fitfully. Her friend Aisling was still in shock from the loss of her mother. Brianna, holding the baby prince, whose blue eyes were alert and looking back at her. She prayed silently to Rhiannon that more had survived and opened the carriage door. "Come with me, we're almost there." She got out and headed for the nearby wrought iron gate.

The others slowly followed her. Tomas's voice came from behind them. "My lady, why are we here?"

She smiled. "This is our safe haven." She regarded the expensive-looking sign on the nearby column as lightning flashed across the sky. Banque Dupris.

Two guards were at the gate as always. She stopped at the bars. "Fy enw i yw Morrigan Bresling, dwi'n mynnu mynediad." My name is Morrigan Bresling, and I demand entry.

The men looked startled for a moment then focused more closely on her. She tried to wait patiently, but her fear and anxiety almost got the best of her. Morrigan's breath caught, she could feel her legs shaking, her vision blurred briefly, and her arm still ached from the wound. One of them opened the small cap on his lantern, signaling the archer tower, while the other opened the gate. She swept past them, with her group of companions close behind her, forcing her walk to hide how weak she felt.

Two more guards opened the Banque Dupris doors as they passed, saluting fists to heart. She nodded, too tired to do much else and went inside, followed by the others. The guard captain was there, and thankfully she recognized him. "Captain Cosgrove, it is good to see you."

He bowed and knelt in front of her, one hand on his sword hilt and the other on his chest, bowing his head slightly. "My lady, thank Rhiannon you're alive. When we heard about your mother, we expected the worst."

Morrigan choked for the briefest of moments before replying, her grief was still new. She hoped her voice didn't convey just how weak she felt. "She's gone, and it hurts more than I can say. We must endure—for Cathyor, the prince, and Trefn Cyfiawnder."

"She was a good woman, and I am sorry." He looked toward Brianna, noting both the sword on her back and the baby in her arms. "You have the prince—our duty holds strong. Anything you need, we are yours." The other men nodded in agreement, saluting with fists to chests. He saw the clumsily bandaged wound on her arm. "My lady, you are hurt."

Morrigan nodded, wiping the tears from her eyes, but she smiled too, it was good to have their support. "It's nothing. Send messengers to every Dupris property in the city. Any women or girls seeking refuge are to be allowed inside. Shield them with your lives."

He nodded and stood. "You heard the lady! To horse, men, send out the word!" Some of the other guardsmen sprang into action immediately, heading for the back door where the stables were. They were good men, which Morrigan was thankful for; she needed them now more than ever.

Morrigan went to the stairs and started up, ignoring the gasps and looks of surprise from those who had joined her out of the darkness. There would be enough time to explain later, once they were safe. Then she stopped for a moment and turned back. "Captain, please find me a biume for the twins and dispatch a guardsman to bring in Tomas's wife. Then send food up for everyone." She looked around the room at her companions and the guardsmen, raising her voice to be heard by them all, despite her pain. "Mae adegau o galedi yn gofyn am ddewisiadau anodd." Times of hardship require hard choices. They all saluted again, fists to heart. "Diolch i chi i gyd, mae eich calonnau yn wir." Thank you all, your hearts are true.

She regarded her wayward companions again. "The rest of you, come with me." Morrigan led her companions upstairs, their steps heavy.

. . . . . .

As Morrigan climbed the stairs, Captain Cosgrove watched, his heart heavy yet hopeful. He smiled sadly as he lowered his fist. Their situation was a hard one. Everything they held dear faced annihilation, but the young lady was definitely her mother's daughter. Maybe they'd all make it out of this after all. It was exactly as she had said: Times of hardship required hard choices. It was a damned shame that such terrible choices fell upon one so young. Children should never have to carry such burdens, but he and his men would do everything in their power to help her.

The young lady needed a biume. He could help with that. He smiled and went to see his wife Fiona, who had arrived a little while ago and was resting in the officer's quarters. On his way there he stopped to send a few more of the guards out to retrieve the other man's wife. Tomas, like Declan himself, had been a servant of the Bresling family for nearly his whole life; he truly hoped the man's wife was alright.

Nights like this made Declan really feel his age, but the Bresling family still needed him. He still couldn't believe that Trefn Cyfiawnder had been nearly wiped out, that Cathyor was falling. It was heartbreaking. He paused for a moment to think before going in to see his wife. There was still hope. He'd recognized the sword being carried by the older woman in the young lady's party; it meant the baby being carried by the old woman was the Ahearne heir. Some of his men had seen it, too. He could tell by their now straightened backs and the gleam in their eyes. He had no idea how the young lady had come to escort the prince and his biume, but it was perhaps the brightest sign of hope Declan had seen that day, for if anyone could protect the young prince, and restore order, it was Morrigan Bresling. The lady might still be young, but her mother was a force. If even half of what Meabh Bresling was had been transferred to her daughter, then there was hope.

. . . . . .

Tomas carefully laid the Bishop twins down on the large bed, then he went to go get bandages for Lady Morrigan. They were in the Banque Dupris's upstairs apartments. Young Aisling was sitting down on the bed near the twins, her eyes still hollowed from hours of weeping. Tomas sighed heavily. Children should never have to face these things.

Brianna had laid the baby prince near the twins, and her old shoulders were slumped as she unstrapped the Ahearne sword from her back and sat down wearily. Tomas retrieved bandages and supplies, then knelt by Lady Morrigan as she sat in a chair by the fireplace and very tiredly placed her mother's sword next to her. "My Lady, thank you for sending them to retrieve my wife, that means more to me than I can say. Please allow me? That needs to be bandaged more properly."

She laid her arm out for him. "Of course, Tomas, you are family, I would never leave any of you." There were tears in her eyes and she looked completely exhausted.

The door opened and a woman with red hair came in. "My Lady? You needed a biume? I am here." She paused to bow gracefully before heading toward the babies. Aisling barely noticed and Brianna made to stand up. But it was Lady Morrigan who held up one hand, while pulling her other away from him and laying it on the hilt of her mother's sword. "Stop. You arrived very quickly. Can I trust you?"

The woman smiled and laughed, then bowed again. "I am Fiona Cosgrove, Declan's wife."

Lady Morrigan smiled, nodding. "Thank you, Fiona. I am sorry for my distrust, but these are perilous times." She placed her hands back where they'd been. "Thank Rhiannon you're here, Fiona. We need you."

Fiona smiled and went to check on the babies.

"Of course, My Lady, I will help in any way I can."

Tomas sighed, his heart heavy. His lady was strong, she certainly was her mother's daughter, but she was still a child. She would need him in the years to come. There would be more work than any one woman, even Morrigan, daughter of Meabh Bresling, was capable of alone to save what was left of Cathyor and Trefn Cyfiawnder. He looked up at her while gently wrapping the bandages around her forearm. Morrigan had closed her eyes and was leaning her head slightly forward, resting it upon her other hand. Tomas hoped she was able to get some rest—they all needed it after today, but her especially, because everything depended upon her now. Her breathing slowed and a fragile peace settled over her young face, making him smile.

Chapter Six:
Yr Hyn Sydd ar Ôl
(What Remains)

Marged reined in her new horse at the tree line's crest. Below, Brynn burned. Her night had been spent weeping in the hands of Aerona. Hands trembling on the reins, she felt weak with sorrow and exhaustion. Her life had become a nightmare, but she had needed to do something. Llewellyn women were not made to weep uselessly into their pillows. So, when she had woken earlier this morning, laying on a bed of moss next to a freshwater spring, and seen the horse tied to a nearby tree, she made a hard choice. Marged had decided to ride for Brynn, in the vain hope that she could do something.

The early dawn sun was just cresting over the higher hills around Brynn as Marged looked toward the city. Regret struck her like a sudden pain deep in her heart, and all she could see was terror. The capital—her home, her people, her kingdom—was burning. Aedonians and their Jhorian allies moved about with impunity. They were kicking in doors, executing the few living souls they found, and piling loot in the streets.

Their magic had failed them, her people were done, and now Marged lacked the energy to even wonder how it all happened. Despair gripped her, and she collapsed in the saddle, crying like a child until time blurred as tears fell.

Marged sat back up, but refused to look at the city, instead she turned her horse away. There was nothing she could do, she was too late, and it was all gone. She had failed in her duty as Dduwies Rhyfel, one of Trefn Cyfiawnder's Goddesses of War—their order's most elite warriors. Her Dryad, Aerona, had forgiven her and gave Marged leave to go; the horse was proof enough of that. How could she ever forgive herself for surviving, when everyone and everything she loved was gone? She couldn't look heartbreak in the face again. That meant it was time to go. But to where?

Somewhere without war and soldiers, without violence and blood. Without failure and heartbreak. Never again. Marged took off the torn cloak she'd found and stared at the Coeden Gysegredig, or "Sacred Tree," symbol on its front and sword of Trefn Cyfiawnder. The Order of Justice, her sisters, and her life—all of it was gone. A gust of wind caught the cloak, and she let it go, watching it fall and blow away along the ground.

Marged snapped the horse's reins and started moving. As the horse's hooves broke the soil, her mind drifted to better times and the battle pledge she and her sisters used to scream, not knowing its true meaning.

Peidiwch byth ag ofni'r cwymp, oherwydd yfory, fel hadau ein hynafiaid, byddwn yn codi eto. She knew its meaning now, all too well, and she was afraid they would never rise again.

. . . . . .

It was early morning when Morrigan turned from the city's ruin to watch the lone supply wagon as it faded from sight into a distant fog as the road turned away into a forest. Most of the city was still burning behind her. She could hear shouting, the occasional building collapse, and combat in nearly every direction, but none of it was close to her. She and the Dupris family properties were protected by their house guard. There was a retinue of them with her, which made their small group safer than most.

The previous day and night had been a horrendous affair, but they were safe and Morrigan had sent every spare guard she could to protect any woman or girl they could find. It wasn't enough. Nothing would have been, though, in the face of what had happened. She squeezed Aisling's hand and felt her friend squeeze hers back. Neither of them spoke or looked at one another; they were both watching the wagon. Everything would eventually depend upon that lone wagon, and she could not send anyone with it for fear the Aedonians would realize who it carried.

The wagons were used to supply every House Dupris property throughout Eastern Innatraea, and much as she hated to admit it, being their ally helped now. Many doubted her mother's duplicitous political and financial maneuvering, but it was those very things that would save them all now. This specific wagon, like all of those that served the Dupris properties in Aedonia's capital city of Bethseda, was marked by a golden star, the symbol of Aedonian royalty, making it less likely it would be searched or even slowed down by any soldiers who saw it.

Even if it was, no one would find the small secret chamber inside. Rhiannon protect you, my dear prince. May we meet again someday. Tears welled up in her eyes and her throat tightened as she squeezed Aisling's hand again, but Aisling turned and they embraced one another instead.

Tomas spoke from beside them. "My Lady, where are they going?"

After a few moments, she stepped back from her friend's arms and looked up at him. "It's safer, we don't know. The wagoner will do his job, and Brianna has been in service to House Ahearne for three generations." She felt tears again. "We must have faith in Rhiannon." Morrigan looked at her companions and they all nodded to her, resolute in their belief that she knew what needed to be done. If only she was as certain, but there was no choice—they were all that was left.

Morrigan saw one of the guardsmen lean in to speak quietly to Declan Cosgrove, before stepping back to rejoin the line. "What news from the city, Captain?"

His eyes took on a look of concern. "Most of it is grim or maybe just rumors, My Lady."

"Tell me."

"The king and queen are both dead." He choked and his eyes looked angry. "The king's head is on a pike at the castle gate. Queen Isolde sacrificed herself in an explosion."

Morrigan steeled herself, clenching her fists. "Continue."

"Much of the city is as we saw it, in ruins and burning." He sighed and rubbed his beard. "There are rumors of Trefn Cyfiawnder's magic returning later in the battle, though I cannot lend them much credence."

Morrigan closed her eyes. Their magic had failed them when the invasion began, and she still had no idea why. Aisling squeezed her hand, and she held on tight. "What do you mean, Captain?"

He spoke in a rush. "They say that a woman wielding two magic swords killed an entire squad, including an Inquisitor. Another rumor involves a Dryad coming into Innatraea and engaging the enemy directly. There are also numerous reports of women escaping with their blades' magic, including a woman with red hair from Dduwies Rhyfel."

Her mouth almost quivered into a smile. "I truly hope even half of it proves to be factual, the Aedonians and Jhorians deserve far worse."

The line of guardsmen suddenly cheered. A guardsman came running and stopped in front of the captain and saluted. "Ser, Lady Gwendolyn Drake and the trainees have survived. They're across Lake Rhiannon on the island."

Morrigan smiled now, as a little sadness lifted from her heart. Every woman of Trefn Cyfiawnder that survived was reason enough to celebrate, but Gwendolyn Drake was their Rhyfelfeistr, or "Warmaster," their most feared warrior.

"That is excellent news, guardsman, thank you." She took a deep breath and squeezed her friend's hand again. "We will need her in the days to come." The guardsman saluted and headed back to the line. "Captain, you and your men have performed better than I'd dared to hope. Give all of them promotions."

He saluted, fingers to heart. "Yes, My Lady, thank you."

"And Captain?"

"Yes, My Lady?"

"You are now the commander of my personal guard. Raise our blades as you deem worthy."

He saluted, fingers to heart. "Thank you, My Lady, I shall serve you to the best of my abilities so long as I breathe."

She nodded in respect. "You already have, Commander Cosgrove. Tomas?"

He nodded. "Yes, My Lady?"

"Every rumor we hear will need to be pursued and verified, even those that sound impossible."

"Yes, My Lady, of course."

She sighed as she made yet another difficult decision. "Send word ahead to prepare the estates in Bethseda. We will begin there, as our mothers planned."

Tomas to his credit only looked mildly surprised. "Yes, My Lady. Are you certain?"

Morrigan nodded. "I am. Also everyone will need new names and places to go. Spare nothing."

Tomas nodded and she noted a look of pride in Cosgrove's eyes. "Of course, right away, My Lady."

Morrigan turned around and met Aisling's eyes. "Are you ready? It's time for what our mothers planned. Everything changes now."

Aisling held Morrigan's gaze; sadness and determination warred in her eyes. "I am. Promise me we'll always be there for each other, Morrigan. Promise me..."

Morrigan nodded as they embraced. "I promise. Always, until the end." When they stepped away from each other, Morrigan looked back across the city of Brynn, forcing herself to confront her feelings of loss and anger. Cathyor had fallen. But the Trefn Cyfiawnder would not, so long as she lived.

Morrigan spoke quietly. Promises did not require shouting to be kept. "Peidiwch byth ag ofni'r cwymp, oherwydd yfory, fel hadau ein hynafiaid, byddwn yn codi eto." Never fear the fall. For tomorrow, like the seeds of our ancestors, we will rise again. Commander Cosgrove, Tomas, and the line of guardsmen came to stand by her and Aisling, hands on their hearts, as she continued. "Dydd Dial a Marwolaeth yn dod." The day of vengeance and death is coming.

All their voices joined hers. "Mae Trefn Cyfiawnder yn sefyll." The Order of Justice stands.

. . . . . .

Elspeth closed her eyes, trying to think amidst the chaos of her emotions. She hadn't slept yet. Last night was a nightmare that she only survived because Archibald was with her. He had found a small cart for Brighid's body and stayed with them through it all. They had spent hours navigating burning streets, avoiding enemy patrols, and weeping at every new charnel pile of what their people had been. She breathed deeply, counting her breaths in order to calm herself. A few hours after sunrise, they had finally reached the crest of a hill outside the city and rested.

There, she had spotted a muddied torn Trefn Cyfiawnder cloak on the ground, and a little ways off, horse tracks leading into the forest. In the vain hope of finding someone alive, they followed the tracks but lost them in a stream. She prayed to Rhiannon that whoever they had previously belonged to survived and would find the happy life she deserved.

Then Elspeth had started feeling a gentle pull inside, as if something was calling her. She started following it, only because she didn't know what else to do with everything she was feeling. Wordlessly, Archibald followed her, pulling Brighid's funeral cart behind him. It was tough going. The deep woods weren't made for carts and both of them were exhausted, but they kept on—whether it in hope, desperation, or lack of another choice, she didn't know.

Eventually the path had led them to the base of a giant oak tree, which Elspeth now stood under, holding her sister's sword. She opened her eyes and looked down through fresh tears at the newly covered grave, Brighid's resting place, under that very oak tree.

Elspeth could feel her sister's sword, Gwreichionen, or "Glimmer," pulsing in her hand. Striations of fiery red power flowed along its blade fitfully, seeking release. The sword wanted to stay with Elspeth, to be used by her hand to slay their enemies. But she couldn't keep it. She held too much heartbreak to wield that sword. She had failed. She had not been able to save her king, the prince, her sister Brighid, or even find her sister's daughter Aisling. Everything in her screamed with guilt, rage, and sadness; her body shook with it, her knees threatening to buckle. She stood there holding her dead sister's sword, unable to move. Archibald gently put a hand on her shoulder as she started weeping harder.

After some time, Elspeth knelt and Archibald stepped back, knowing that however difficult it was, this moment was hers alone. She laid her sister's sword out before her and looked at its blade, watching how it caught the light filtering through the tree branches above them. Finally, sighing with a heavy heart, she held it up and slowly—reverently—pushed Glimmer into the freshly disturbed soil in front of Brighid's grave. Elspeth stopped, and closed her eyes, leaning her forehead against the sword's pommel. "Hwyl fawr chwaer, bydded i ti gael heddwch yn y Byd Nesaf." Goodbye, sister, may you find peace in the next world.

Then the sound of tree branches creaking loudly interrupted her silent memorial as a startlingly strong wind blew around her. Elspeth opened her eyes and looked up, already knowing what she would see— her Dryad, Calon, whose name meant Heart, once a comfort, now a wound. She was correct, but there was also a second Dryad, Nerthal, who had been bonded to her sister and whose name meant Strong. Both giants met her gaze; they were only showing half of themselves, as if their body was deep inside Innatraea. They did this sometimes, though it was disconcerting to see.

Nerthal leaned in close, its face nearly touching Elspeth's. Elspeth could sense the Dryad's compassion, but also her incredible anger. "Cymerwch gleddyf Brighid, teithiwn fel un, y tri ohonom." Take Brighid's sword, we will travel as one, the three of us.

Elspeth felt her desire for vengeance, and a part of her wanted to say yes, but she couldn't. Her voice choked as she spoke. "Forgive me, but I cannot endure the pain."

Nerthal's eyes showed a brief flash of anger, but then understanding. Her sister's sword lifted into the air. "Byddwn yn aros i chi. Dydd Dial a Marwolaeth yn dod." We will wait for you. The day of vengeance and death is coming. Her sister's sword burst into flames, before floating into the air and disappearing with Nerthal.

Calon did not speak at first, but her giant arms came out of the ground, passing through it like Innatraea wasn't real. She embraced Elspeth and pulled her close, then the Dryad lowered her forehead and rested it against Elspeth's own. "Rwyf yma. Llefain. Ond gadewch i'r euogrwydd fynd, nid yw'n perthyn i chi." I am here. Cry. But let the guilt go, it does not belong to you.

Chapter Seven:
Gwirionedd
(Truth)

> *"I ddod o hyd i batrwm tynged rhywun*
> *mae'n rhaid i chi yn gyntaf gysoni â'r gwir.*
> *To find the pattern of one's destiny*
> *you must first reconcile with the truth."*
> *-Old Cathyoran Saying*

A few weeks before present day...

Edmond held the cabin door open, lantern aloft, as his grandmother stepped inside. They had stayed at the Al'Shanes' late, as usual; they were all like one big family. Surprisingly, instead of going to her bed, his grandmother sat at their small table and looked at him. "Edmond, light the hearth and come sit with me. It's time we spoke about something."

Curious, Edmond did as she asked without question. His grandmother was getting older, and he often worried about how she would get along after he left for Bethseda.

After lighting the hearth, he filled their small tea kettle and hung it before sitting down. He had recently gotten Seylan black tea, her favorite, loving the small surprise. He sat down and looked at her, placing his hands on the table. "What did you want to talk about?"

His grandmother leaned forward a little and put her hands around his, looking at him. "I'll be alright after you leave. I'll still have Gertrude, Crilla, and Marged. You don't need to worry."

Edmond nodded, of course she knew that he'd been thinking about it, yet her eyes said there was more. "I know, but I still worry about you. There's something else you wanted to talk about, is there not?"

She closed her eyes for a moment, then looked out the window before meeting his eyes again. "Yes. I know Marged had you wrap your sword." She looked at it and smiled. "It's good that you listened to her. Did she tell you why?"

He frowned. Maybe that meant he was finally going to get some answers about where he came from. "Just that it's a special sword and certain people may cause trouble for me if they see it. Is that what you wanted to talk about?"

She squeezed his hands tighter and sighed heavily. "Not exactly, but it is related." She looked at him directly and he saw love there, like always, but there was also sadness and guilt. "Edmond, I am not your grandmother."

Edmond's hands tensed, and his breath caught, as he felt panic creep into his voice. "What are you talking about?!"

Brianna closed her eyes as she started speaking again, there were tears on her cheeks now. "Your parents, they were a very small Cathyoran house—royalty, but not influential. I was their biume. My duty was to protect you." She opened her eyes and met his gaze. There was a plea for forgiveness there. "When the Jhorians attacked, your parents ordered me to flee, to take you and the sword to safety. I kept this a secret until now to protect you. Forgive me, Edmond—please?"

Edmond stayed quiet for a few moments before replying, looking out the window himself now, starting to feel lost. Brianna had lied to him. She wasn't his grandmother, but she loved him—had even given her life to protect and raise him. "What was my family's name?"

She wiped her eyes and looked at him, her emotions obviously still raw. "Carlon. I took the name when we came here so that you could keep it and not raise suspicion."

Edmond nodded and looked around their small cabin, searching for something, though he didn't know what. His gaze settled on his sword, a relic of his father—or so he'd been told.

"My sword?"

"It belonged to your father. A last remnant of how strong the house used to be. It was always passed from father to son." Her eyes focused sharply and she looked at him again. "It is your legacy, Edmond, but it's also dangerous, and partly why I waited so long to tell you the truth. Your family was nobility. Be careful who you trust or show yourself to. You must remain safe. Please."

So that's why Marged sometimes looked at him strangely and told him to wrap his sword's hilt and pommel. She was also worried for his safety and didn't want him to suffer. He pulled his hands away and stood up, which made his grandmother look at him questioningly. He forced a smile, his voice soft. "I forgive you, and I am trying to understand, but I need some time to myself."

He went to the door and opened it.

"Edmond?"

He turned back and their eyes met.

"I love you."

Edmond nodded before replying, "I love you too, grandmother," and walked out into the dark night.

. . . . . .

After Edmond left, Brianna rose, poured herself a cup of tea, and sat back down at their small table with a heavy heart. She had finally told Edmond the truth, a version of it anyway, one that would hopefully give him strength and keep him safe. She was afraid that if Edmond knew he was Prince Cian, he would chase a crown lost to ash. Cathyor was gone, and there was no one left to help him. Even the one surviving member of Trefn Cyfiawnder, Marged Llewellyn, had found another life.

She sipped her favorite tea, seeking to drown the guilt in its aroma and flavor. Had she done enough to protect him? Had Marged and Johnathan trained him well enough? She put her teacup down, sighing heavily. It had to be enough. Her time was coming to an end and he would be on his own soon, she could feel it in her bones.

Brianna took another sip of tea while looking out the window, lost in thought. She loved them all—Taran, Cormac, Cian—cherishing their first steps and words. Tears streamed down her cheeks. There was no throne for Edmond to ascend, the past was gone. She blinked her eyes free of tears and wiped them with the palms of her hands. He was alive, and that would have to be enough.

A creak at the cabin door broke her reverie and she looked up, expecting to see her grandson returning. But it was Marged Llewellyn instead. The woman smiled and gently closed the door before sitting at the small table across from her.

"Brianna. I came to see what you will tell him before he leaves, but judging by the look on his face when I saw him on my way here, I think you already made your choice." Her eyes softened as their gazes met. "It must have been hard. How did he handle it?"

Brianna smiled sadly and nodded. "I told him a version of the truth, and he handled it well, all things considered. He has a strong heart."

Marged's look became one of cautious curiosity as she clasped her hands together. "A *version* of the truth?"

"Yes, I told him he's from House Carlon, a small noble house, killed only by Jhorians."

Marged nodded, relief easing her features. "Good—may that keep him safe from danger." She looked out the window. "Cathyor is gone. There is no need to raise old ghosts or die for a dead kingdom." She patted Brianna's hand gently. "That must have been heavy, hiding all that pain."

Brianna nodded in agreement. "That is why I too hope it will be enough. The thought of him having a good life is enough for my heart. Am I right in assuming you will stay here with your husbands?"

Marged nodded gently. "Yes. Aliselle Falls is my home now and those two saved me. They are my heart. I truly wish Edmond the best, but I will not go with him."

Brianna reached across the table and squeezed Marged's hands. "I understand. Happiness is hard to find in this life. You are choosing wisely. Thank you for telling me." Suddenly she felt tired, as if the last of her energy was almost gone. She stood up slowly and started to shuffle to her bed, but her steps faltered. Marged joined her, lending an arm for support.

Once Brianna was lying down, Marged gently put a blanket over her and smiled. "You did well with Edmond. He is a good man." Marged brushed her face with gentle fingers. "He may not know it, but he is an Ahearne to his core."

Brianna smiled with quiet joy, the tea's warmth lingered, and she closed her eyes for the last time. Marged lowered her face, closing her own eyes, to cry softly. Brianna had been the last other Cathyoran woman in her life, and now she was gone. "Hwyl fawr chwaer, bydded i ti gael heddwch yn y Byd Nesaf." Goodbye, sister, may you find peace in the next world.

CHAPTER EIGHT: THE SHEPHERD KING

Present day...

Edmond stood up. His legs ached from days on the road, and he slung the fish over his shoulder, alongside his sword and knapsack. He gazed across the highway at the Shepherd King, the Great Tree he'd been walking toward for days since parting ways with Jonaas and Rosalie. This was his first time really being alone in his life, and he hated it—the silence gnawed at him. It made him start thinking about his grandmother, his past before Aliselle Falls, and his friends who were now on their own journeys.

He crossed the road toward the giant tree. He decided to camp by it, because his friends would have wanted to see it. They were always interested in Innatraea's history, and strange things like magic, the Great

Trees, and stories of older times. Edmond missed them and they would have both loved to see this, so here he was.

He paused, gazing up at the tree's towering trunk that seemed to go up into the clouds. It really was an amazing sight, even if he hadn't thought about it in the same way as his friends had while growing up. It was hard to believe such giant things existed in the world when you lived in a farm town like Aliselle Falls. He chuckled ruefully when he caught himself thinking like them and pressed on with his trek. It was getting late and he needed to cook his fish before bedding down for the night.

As Edmond neared the hill's crest, flute notes and singing drifted toward him. He smiled; there must be a group of shepherds nearby. He remembered that Jonaas' book had said that shepherds often used the great tree as a gathering place when tending their flocks. He decided to head that way. Maybe he'd be lucky to come across some friendly folk and wouldn't have to eat his fish alone. There was always the question of whether you could trust fellow travelers on the road, but from growing up around people like Jonaas, he'd learned that those who treated their animals well were generally more trustworthy than most.

When Edmond reached the hill's crest, he stopped to look ahead, through the distance between himself and the tree. There was a large flock of sheep wandering around the fields, and near them a small camp made of several wagons and a single campfire, where he could see people singing and playing their shepherd's pipes.

As he came closer, a tall, barrel-chested man, bearded and scraggly-haired, gripped a wickedly hooked staff and stood up to watch him, as two others nearer the flock raised and nocked their bows. Edmond stopped walking and raised his arms, displaying his string of caught fish.

"Ho the camp. I'm just looking for a fire to share my catch and some camaraderie. I mean no harm."

The tall man eyed him up and down, then nodded, which caused the others to lower their bows. "I'm Basaraba. You're welcome to join our fire in peace. Come, what's your name and where did you travel from?"

Edmond didn't like the idea of sharing where he was from with complete strangers, but they were shepherds and just wanted to know he was safe. "My name is Edmond. I come from a farm town called Aliselle Falls, and I'm headed to Bethseda."

As Edmond drew nearer to their campfire, a very large tan-colored dog emerged from the nearby bushes and approached him, so he held his hand out. The dog regarded him for a moment and walked away toward the flock. Basaraba gave a rough chuckle, lowering his staff to reach out his hand so they could shake. "Well met, young Edmond. Find a spot by the fire and we'll get your fish cooking after our deer is done."

As Edmond sat down, Basaraba pointed around the campfire, saying his companions' names as he did. "Enoh, Andrejan, Matos, my wife Stevana, and Toman. The two lads with the flock, who almost turned you into a lady's pincushion, are Beshim and my son Nicolai."

Edmond smiled, nodding along with the names as he tried to remember them by matching each face to each name. "Well met, all—my thanks for your fire."

Andrejan looked over. He was younger than most at the fire, though still older than Edmond. "What takes you to Bethseda? It's a treacherous place."

Briefly, Edmond considered not telling them the truth. Shepherds were generally not fond of soldiers, but he'd already said where he was from, and his grandmother, even given her lie, had taught him to be honest. And as Jonaas and Rosalie used to always remind him: Changing things for the better requires an Innatraean to first be true to themselves, even when others wouldn't approve—especially in that case, actually. Shepherds loathed the Aedonian military, but honesty outweighed their scorn. "I plan on enlisting."

The man's demeanor changed immediately. "No one sensible does that. That lot of miserable bastards don't believe in a free life."

Basaraba replied, looking a bit amused. "Ease off, not everyone thinks the same way we do. Did you not see the sword on his back?"

"No, that's alright. A man should be able to defend his own choices when asked." Edmond put his elbows on his knees and clasped his hands under his chin before speaking further. "Perhaps more sensible men should."

Andrejan's eyebrows arched in disbelief. "Sensible men don't stand by and do nothing." He looked around the camp. "Taking care of your family and friends, caring for animals and your way of life, that counts for doing something."

Edmond clenched his right fist and stared into the fire, his eyes narrowing and jaw tightening. "I don't have a family anymore and my friends have their own paths, but I can still do good for Innatraea. The Aedonian military can be cruel. I've seen their injustice since leaving home." He met Andrejan's eyes. "I plan on changing that." Edmond looked back into the fire a moment later, feeling a bit embarrassed for saying such strong words, but it was what he believed.

Andrejan stroked his beard, lost in thought, but it was Basaraba who replied. "Do you really think one young man can make a difference? That is a mighty big challenge."

Edmond nodded. It was a big challenge and sometimes the idea of facing it felt heavy, but a man had to have courage for what he believed in. "I think it's the only difference that matters. Most battles depend on the will of a few men, or even only one man."

One of the other men interjected. Edmond thought his name was Toman. "Battle?"

Edmond met the man's eyes. "What else do you call a man standing up for right in a troubled world?"

Basaraba smiled as he stood up to help Enoh remove their deer from the fire to make room for Edmond's fish. "You are an interesting young man, well met."

Stevana edged closer. Her lilting voice danced with amusement. "You have quite a big head for someone so young. Your upbringing must've been among lively souls."

Enoh laughed. "Big head? He's a light-blinded fool if he thinks one young man can make such a difference in the world."

Edmond laughed in response, which seemed to take his new companions by surprise. Maybe they expected more of an argument. But this was life. Not everyone agreed, and it was good to be amongst fellow Innatraeans again. "My grandmother always said one woman or man's will can change Innatraea."

. . . . . .

A few days later Basaraba was leaning against his shepherd's crook, watching their flock, lost in thought. He often found himself doing this in recent years, maybe it was a part of getting older? It was not as often that his thoughts drifted to things other than his family, friends, and their flock. Edmond's words played through his mind again. "My grandmother always said one woman or man's will can change Innatraea." Shepherds never saw themselves shaping Innatraea, yet their leader's choices brought them fortune or doom. Did the young man mean that? He ran a hand through his beard with a sigh. These thoughts weren't really a part of a shepherd's life, but he'd become more prone to thinking them in recent years.

Stevana's hands wrapped around him as she leaned against him. "You have been lost in your thoughts more than usual lately, old man. What is it that's bothering you?"

Basaraba smiled and leaned his head gently against hers. "It's what that young man Edmond said." He scanned their flock again as he spoke. "Every flock and shepherd's band has a leader, whose decisions can bring fortune or doom. Do you think all of Innatraea is like that?" He laughed ruefully, amused at himself for speaking such thoughts. "Such thoughts stray beyond a shepherd's lot—yet I wonder."

Stevana laughed too, in her lilting way that always made him smile. "They do." She came around to face him, putting a hand on his cheek, meeting his eyes. "But I didn't marry you because you're a shepherd, my love." She gently stroked his cheek. "I married you because you're a leader, with a good heart, and thoughts worthy of something greater."

Basaraba smiled happily. "How do you always know the answers, my love?"

She patted his cheek and turned to watch their flock with him. Her voice sounded amused. "Because I am a woman."

The wind picked up, sending his wife's hair flowing in the air and giving him a chill. Basaraba used his free hand to close his cloak tighter around himself. He couldn't help but feel as though something in the wind was different lately, as though change was coming their way. His gaze swept their flock again, seeking the vague threat he felt deep in his bones. He decided to make a joke, hoping to lighten the heaviness he was feeling. "Yes, our flock has their ewe, and we have my wife!"

Stevana looked at him sideways and smiled while tying her hair back. "The wind's grown strange, my love—I feel it too."

They watched their flock in silence for a little while after that. If his wife felt it, then he wasn't just worrying about nothing. Innatraea was changing, and the wind knew. He couldn't help but wonder if Edmond had something to do with it.

CHAPTER NINE:
CERDDED Y BONT
(WALKING THE BRIDGE)

"Mae gwir arweinwyr yn adeiladwyr pontydd.
True leaders are bridge builders."
-Old Cathyoran Saying

Edmond trudged on, his shoulders slumped. Walking wasn't a hard thing to do, but his boots felt heavier than usual. It had been a few days since his evening amongst Basaraba and the other shepherds. Days more since leaving Jonaas and Rosalie. And weeks since losing his grandmother. They all weighed heavily on his mind still. He stopped and looked back at the Shepherd King. He could still see the giant tree in the distance behind him, even after a few days of walking.

Truthfully, he already missed being amongst people, and especially traveling with his friends, but Edmond knew he was doing the right thing. Something inside of him screamed he was headed to where he was meant to be. He remembered the old phrase he'd said to Rosalie not long ago, "Let your feet follow your heart until you find your place of resurrection." His grandmother had told him that his parents had been nobility, that they were from Cathyor, and to him that meant he was meant for better things.

He knew Cathyor was gone, but he still felt like his destiny was there, that something was pulling him toward it. Whether it was his heart, his soul, or fate, he rarely pondered such mysteries. All he knew for certain was that every step he took brought him closer to that sense of purpose and further away from the grief of finding out where he'd come from, losing his grandmother and saying goodbye to his friends. It was like a battle inside of him, leaving his old life behind and heading toward a new one, fighting his way out from under grief's shadow.

A phrase Marged had taught him came to mind: "Gallwch chi golli brwydrau neu ryfeloedd, ond peidiwch byth â gadael i'ch calon gael ei threchu." She'd taught him enough of what she called the old tongue— that he now suspected was Cathyoran—for him to understand what it meant. You can lose battles or wars but never let your heart be defeated. In war speed was victory; once you found yourself where your opponent expected you it was over. Edmond broke into a run.

Coming over the next hill, he eased to a halt. Running was harder loaded down with his pack, sword, and heavy traveler's boots. There also seemed to be something happening ahead. A small group of people were clustered around a wagon that looked like it was stuck in the mud just off the King's Highway. Edmond nodded and started heading their way. He wasn't a knight yet but one didn't just become chivalrous upon earning a title. According to his grandmother, helping others was a way of life.

The small group was a farmer, his wife, and their two young daughters. The man saw Edmond and brandished a rough-hewn cudgel his way. "We don't want any trouble, young man. Just keep walking."

Edmond stopped and held his hands up. "I don't mean any harm. What happened here?"

The woman put her arms around the two girls protectively as the man crossed his arms and looked at Edmond skeptically. He dipped his head, deeming him no foe. "A battalion of soldiers ran our cart off the road on their way north." His scornful tone bared his disdain, which was also probably why they were eyeing Edmond so carefully. He did have a sword strapped to his back, after all.

Edmond could tell that the farmer's anger was showing; his eyes kept darting nervously to the woman and two girls, then back to him. Edmond tried to calm his voice. "I'm sorry that happened. Soldiers should know better than to harass their populace." He looked at the cart then met the farmer's eyes. "Would you allow me to assist you in getting your cart out?"

The man started to nervously rub his hands together and glanced at the woman and two girls again. The woman spoke first, while ushering their two girls and pulling their horse away from the cart. "Come now, Herbert, he's not going to hurt us, and we need the help."

Herbert nodded and ceased his fidgeting, which Edmond was thankful for. He didn't like to make people nervous, unless of course they deserved it. He grinned and knelt to inspect their cart. Finally getting a good look at the wheel, he sighed; it was well and truly stuck. "We're going to need a good-sized tree limb to help leverage the wheel out." He looked around for a moment and spotted a nearby copse of trees, pointing in its direction while he spoke. "I'll go look for something we can use. That way you can stay by the girls. I'll be right back!"

. . . . . .

Gisella glanced past her husband at Edmond, who had helped them again. They were all walking back toward their farm and the town now. Herbert had said one of the cart's axles had cracked but he was good at repairing such things and they weren't far from home. The young man was tall and strong, with pretty blue eyes. She was, not for the first time, glad that her two daughters were not yet old enough to chase after boys. This young man was going to be a heartbreaker. Few men who carried a sword and were so handsome also had good hearts.

She wondered again where he was going and where he'd come from, so she decided to ask him. "Thank you again for helping us. We would have been very badly off without our cart." She looked at her daughters again, both happily sitting in the cart, with their supplies and smiled. "What path brings you here?" Her husband looked her way but said nothing. He knew how curious she was, plus this would make a good story to tell their friends.

Edmond glanced over and smiled. "I'm on my way to Bethseda, to enlist and hopefully become a knight one day."

Herbert raised his brow at the young man, then spoke in a salty voice. "That's an odd choice of occupation, given your reaction to what those soldiers did to our cart."

Gisella smacked him. He had a habit of saying the darndest things at times. "Herbert!" Though she supposed he did have a point. "You will have to excuse my husband. Though he does raise a curious notion. Why are you joining the Aedonian military?"

"Once, I'd have given a different answer, but now it's to show them that they must do better." Edmond looked down momentarily while speaking. His words had come out quietly and with purpose, like there was true weight behind them.

A feeling came over Gisella, as if they were part of something important, something that truly mattered. There were very few of those in the lives of ordinary Innatraeans, and it was apparently affecting Herbert as well, because his gaze softened as he rubbed his beard thoughtfully for a few moments before replying. "Admirable, lad. What difference can one man make?" Gisella wanted to smack him again, but his salty tone was gone this time; he just wasn't the best with words.

"My friend might've said a single flame lights others. But my grandmother always said one woman or man's will can change Innatraea." Edmond rubbed his chin, his brow furrowed thoughtfully before continuing, did all men do that? "When I first left home, I just wanted the glory of being a knight. Battles, skill, respect, wealth, and all. But since then, some of the things I've seen have made me think. The commoners of any kingdom should never fear its soldiers, that's wrong. So, I want to do something about it."

Gisella studied him, struck by the dedication in his voice. "They sound like very wise people, your grandmother and your friends. What did you see that changed your purpose so much?"

"Rosalie and Jonaas, I grew up with them. They were some of the smartest and kindest people I knew back home in Aliselle Falls. My grandmother was the same." He paused for a moment, looking thoughtful again. "As to what I saw, it was much the same as your cart back there. Soldiers mistreating the people they're supposed to protect, and those same people being afraid." He nodded to himself. "I was taught that a knight's job is to be the bridge between nobility and common folk, not harass them."

Gisella couldn't help but smile, as that same feeling of something important came over her again. "I think you do just fine with words and both your friends and grandmother would be proud of you. I hope you do well, Edmond, thank you again for helping us."

Herbert patted Tawney, their horse, to make her stop before they started up the path to their farm. They clasped hands. Herbert's face tinged with sheepishness. "Thank you for helping us, lad. Our farm is this way." He pointed down the road a bit further. "You'll find Talberston's Crossing down the road over there. We don't have much in the way of spare food or room. But tell Bernard at the Feather and Quill our names, and he'll take good care of you."

Edmond nodded very politely. "Thank you, take care of yourselves."

Gisella offered a final smile as their paths diverged. "Take care, young man, I truly hope you accomplish everything you spoke of."

Her daughters, Amelia and Sarai, both waved goodbye too, as they started heading home. Gisella turned back for a moment to watch the young man disappear around the bend toward town. Interarea had shifted, the wind whispered it so. It was more than freeing a cart—a bridge was built between them. She could feel it, and so could her husband, because Herbert also stopped to watch Edmond, while rubbing his beard thoughtfully. She would have to remember the young man's name.

CHAPTER TEN: TALBERSTON'S CROSSING

*"Y mae y rhai o wir uchelwyr yn ceisio llais yr
Innatraeaniaid cyffredin ym mhob peth.
Those of true nobility seek the voice of common
Innatraeans in all things."*
-Old Cathyoran Saying

Edmond paused, eyeing Talberston's Crossing, a medium sized town, bigger than Aliselle Falls, but dwarfed by Haversfjord. The place seemed to be dominated by inns, stables, warehouses, and the docks where he saw ships and their sailors constantly moving. He welcomed this bustle; towns like these had inns for every traveler, he knew. When Herbert had first mentioned the Feather and Quill, Edmond instantly pictured one of those posh lady's inns like the one Rosalie had tried to stick them with back in Haversfjord. There was nothing wrong with them, but he definitely preferred a different style of lodging. He shuddered as he recalled The Lady's Feather, then chuckled at his own folly and continued into town.

As he entered Talberston's Crossing, Edmond sidestepped a few moving carts and jumped onto the walkway of a nearby merchant's shop to avoid a group of horses, weaving around many people going about their day. Many might chafe at this, yet he reveled in it. He paused briefly to savor the clamor of everyday Innatraeans going about their daily tasks. Having people around him helped distract him from thoughts about his grandmother and not being with his friends anymore. Traveling alone was definitely not for him. Hopefully his journey to Bethseda wouldn't last much longer.

After asking the food vendor he'd bought a meat pie from, both because he was hungry and the man was reluctant to give directions without a purchase, Edmond rounded a corner and caught sight of the Feather and Quill. He stopped abruptly and the rest of his meat pie fell to the ground as he recoiled. The door of another inn in front of him opened to a loud ruckus inside.

A vaguely familiar-looking Aedonian soldier came out, dragging a woman who appeared to be a barmaid by her arm. Edmond stepped in without even thinking. Where he grew up men didn't treat women like that. He pushed himself in between the two and shoved the man away while pulling the woman's arm out of his grasp. "Hey, what's this about?"

The soldier was furious. He gripped his sword and half-drew it. "I remember you from Haversfjord—got lucky then, huh?"

Edmond's mind raced, recalling previous events in a jumble of images and voices. Marged's was first: "Wrap your sword in twine and sturdy cloth, so that no one sees the hilt. I'll show you how..." Then came Brianna's: "Your family was nobility, be careful who you trust or show yourself to..." The Haversfjord encounter: cutting a soldier's sword, the reeve's questions about his past... He was getting closer to Bethseda. It was time to be more careful, but he also needed to end this quickly before anyone got hurt. In an instant, Edmond sprang at the man without drawing his sword.

Thankfully the surprise move, though foolhardy, worked and his shoulder collided with the man's chest, sending him sprawling into the muddy street. Then his mistake hit him—not when the man rose, swearing, but as the inn door opened again, followed by the unmistakable sound of armor and boots. Soldiers rarely traveled alone.

Edmond stepped to the side and backed up, while raising his hands and trying to keep everyone in view. The man in the street was stomping toward him with a grim look on his face. Four other soldiers, who looked familiar, were taking in the situation with a mixture of amusement and affront. The woman had already fled back into the inn, wisely not wanting any further trouble.

"Now men, I'm sure we all don't want any more trouble. Let's just all go our separate ways?" Edmond appeased.

The man he'd knocked down was nearing him now and Edmond could see the men advancing on his side too. The man flexed his hands and smiled, but there was no humor in his look. "Too late, you cursed dandy."

Anger surged within Edmond. It was one thing for his friends to call him that jokingly, but another for a random soldier he didn't know to do so, especially when he had just been trying to help a woman. "Just back away. I don't want to hurt any of you."

Edmond reached for his sword, but the soldiers were already too close—one of them seized his hand on the hilt. "There'll be none of that here, boy. Talberston's Crossing doesn't have a city watch to save you either. Time to learn your place." The man's fist hit Edmond in the gut, causing him to grunt in pain.

The man sneered a laugh as Edmond fought against the two men who had grabbed him. "You ain't going anywhere this time, boy. Just accept the beating."

Edmond tried to break free again as another soldier came out of the inn. This one Edmond recognized for sure; it was the one whose sword he'd broken in Haversfjord. The man grinned wickedly. "You? Hold him, men. I want to get a few licks in and maybe get myself a new sword, too."

Edmond kept struggling but there were just too many of them, and they were all trained soldiers. He grunted in pain again and his knees buckled as the man whose sword he'd broken punched him in the gut. The others didn't let go. He couldn't help but remember something Marged said before leaving home: "Sometimes one must accept defeat in order to survive." They wouldn't get satisfaction of him crying out in pain, though, no matter what they did.

Blows kept coming, and Edmond felt his strength wane, but his mouth shut, taking their assault as best he could. After some time, they let go by tossing him into the street before surrounding him. The one whose sword he'd broken knelt by Edmond and put a hand on his sword hilt. "Now then, boy, I don't think you'll be needing this anymore."

But another man's voice interrupted, and the man stopped immediately. "Stand down, men." It was the sergeant at arms from days ago, his white tabard and armor glinting as he crouched by Edmond while the other man moved away. Edmond felt himself drifting as the man spoke. "You earned that thrashing for crossing my men, but we are not thieves."

· · · · · ·

Irmina sighed and doused the young man with a bucket of cold water before setting it down. He was lying in the dirt outside her inn, after having been beaten very soundly by the soldiers. Normally she wouldn't care, young fools got what they deserved mostly, but he had helped save Diofrit from what would have most likely been worse. She believed that one act of kindness always deserved another, even if he was likely to be a pain in her backside.

She stepped away a short distance as the young man quickly sat up, swinging his arms, then grabbing his sword hilt; its presence seemed to relax him a little. Some men were better than others, but inside, many of them held the same habits. "Yes, they left your sword and coin. Their sergeant came to see what was happening and didn't abide his men descending into common thievery."

She got a better look at him as he replied groggily to her. He wasn't just young and foolish but also way too pretty for his own good. "Thank you, m'lady, for the timely, though wet, wake up."

He started to get up but grunted in pain and sat back down, so Irmina moved closer and extended her hand to aid him. He didn't seem like the dangerous type and had gotten into this situation by helping Diofrit, which indicated good character. "Come on, up with you. A young man shouldn't be laying in the dirt."

He grimaced in obvious pain while taking her hand to help himself up. She couldn't help but notice he was heavier than she thought, probably because of his muscular build. She had to lean back while pulling him up to avoid being pulled over herself. He also seemed to accept her help without any reservation toward his manhood, an odd quality in any man let alone one so young.

Once he found his legs, the young man tried to stretch and feel out his injuries, but he immediately gasped in pain before swaying gently. It took him a moment to catch his breath, but he still tried to smile. "Thank you again, m'lady, for your assistance."

She smiled back at him. "You are welcome, young man. You're in no condition to travel. Do you have an inn in town already?"

He was becoming more alert but was still obviously woozy. "I do not, but Gisella and Herbert said to find their friend at the Feather and Quill. I helped them with their cart on the King's Highway outside of town."

"That travesty of an inn? Nonsense, you'll stay here with us at The Drunken Bear. I am the proprietress, and you did manage to rescue one of my girls, even if it earned you a beating. Come along and tell me your name. I am Irmina."

He looked in the direction of the Feather and Quill and took a shaky step, but stopped again, swaying in pain. It was an interesting display—not because he knew where he was going; directions were easy enough to come by—but because he felt a certain loyalty to the place he'd been sent by those he'd helped. He was definitely a different sort than she was used to. She huffed and slipped her arm beneath his shoulder to help him walk, to which he flashed a sheepish grin. "Thank you again, m'lady. My name is Edmond."

She was once again surprised at how easily he accepted her help. Grunting in pain, they neared her inn's door, and she decided she might as well ask him about his behavior—answering questions might distract him from his hurt. "You seem very accepting of a woman's help. That is unusual here in Aedonia. Where are you from?"

He started to laugh but stopped, choking in obvious pain, before replying quietly. "In my home town, women stand as equal and as fierce as men, even though it's within Aedonia's borders. I suppose it was an exception, but one I am glad of."

She would have to ask him about his hometown later when she had time and he was more alert, because there was no hurry judging by his groggy swaying movements and grunts of pain. She couldn't resist noting the fine sinew of his muscular body as she helped him step through the entryway of her inn. She shook her head gently and laughed to herself. He was young enough to be her son, but she looked at his back side anyway; it had been a few years since her Nathanael had passed.

Chapter Eleven:
Irmina

"Calon gwraig yw ei chryfder.
A woman's heart is her strength."
-Old Cathyoran Saying

The cabin burned with his grandmother inside—dead. Yet suddenly she stood before him, and he burned within the flames too. "Edmond, I am not your grandmother." Her lined face flared with flame. "They are a small Cathyoran house, royalty..."

Edmond jolted awake, his breath ragged. Pain throbbed in his ribs, everything else hurt too, and he wasn't sure where he was. When he tried to sit up his body protested in pain and a very firm hand gently pushed him back down. He sighed resignedly, tilting his head up enough to look around. His eyes almost immediately fell upon a woman sitting next to him on the bed. She was older than him by a few decades, but was still quite attractive, with sharp green eyes and blond hair tied up into a bun. She wordlessly arched an eyebrow at him as he laid his head back down. He closed his eyes, attempting to banish the nightmare from his mind while also trying to remember why she looked familiar... She had helped him in the street after his altercation with the soldiers. What had her name been? He opened his eyes and looked at her again, trying to smile confidently. "Thank you again, m'lady."

She smiled at him, amused. "If I had a gold mark for every time you've said that I could buy a second inn."

As she was speaking, Edmond realized he could feel her hand against his bare skin. He looked down and saw that his chest was bruised and cut, though bandaged, above the blankets that covered his waist and legs. Worse, he could tell that he wasn't wearing anything under the blankets. She'd taken his clothes. His gaze snapped wide. "I'm naked!"

She just smiled, even more amused. She gently patted his cheek with her hand, leaving the other on his chest. "Relax, young Edmond. I had to bandage your wounds and apply ointment. Besides, you are far from the only unclothed man I have seen in my life."

"My clothes? My sword?"

She motioned to another part of the room with her eyes, which were still twinkling with amusement. "Do not worry, they are there."

Edmond followed her gaze by turning his head slowly and saw his things arranged neatly in a chair against the far wall. He sighed, feeling slightly more at ease, until a keen ache stabbed his chest. He looked back at her, suddenly remembering her name. "What are you doing, Irmina?"

Irmina's fingers lingered on his chest, where she had been removing one of his bandages. "What happened to 'm'lady'?"

He coughed and immediately felt a spasm of pain.

She tapped his cheek with soft care. "It's alright, a woman likes it when an attractive young man knows her name." She held up a small glass bottle. "I have to administer more ointment and change your bandages."

Edmond tried to relax a little. He was still in a lot of pain, and she was just trying to help him, even though the whole situation was incredibly awkward. Was she touching him just a little longer than necessary? Or was she just cleaning his wounds and administering ointment while bandaging him back up, like she said? "Thank you again, Irmina. I appreciate your kindness."

Irmina's hand stilled as she spread the pungent balm onto his skin and muscles, around one of the larger bruises. A shiver raced through him as she spoke, smiling. "You saved Diofrit from a lot worse, I think, and one act of kindness always deserves another."

"Rosalie would say something like that."

Her hand seemed to tense—or was he delirious? "Who is Rosalie?"

"She was a girl I knew back home."

Irmina's eyes seemed to focus a little more intently on his. "Your childhood love?"

"What?! No. She and Jonaas were each other's childhood loves. We all just grew up together." There were a few seconds of silence, then he gasped as a sharp pang from one of the cuts she was bandaging shot through him. "We all separated recently, in Haversfjord. Jonaas is headed toward Royal Seyla and Rosalie is bound for Sceotan."

"There." Irmina secured the bandage and wiped her hands with a cloth. "You keep very interesting friends, Edmond. What about you? Where are you headed that brought you this way?"

"I'm going to Bethseda, to enlist."

She met his eyes again. "I see, on your way to play soldier along with the other young men."

"No, it's more than that..."

Irmina's eyes twinkled with amusement and she smiled before patting his cheek again. "Rest now, you'll be with us for at least a few weeks to heal. A soldier needs to be in good health." She stood up and looked at him. He couldn't tell what the look in her eyes meant. "Don't get dressed or try to move again too soon."

Edmond watched her walk to the door of the small room. He couldn't help but notice the sway of her hips and the bold confidence she showed in her stride. Something about her reminded him of Marged. As Irmina opened the door to leave, he spoke. "Thank you again, m'lady."

Irmina nodded and smiled at him. "We're back to 'm'lady' again, are we? You're very welcome, Edmond. Get some sleep." With that she was gone and he closed his eyes, realizing how tired he actually was.

. . . . . .

After she closed the door, Irmina leaned against it quietly and sighed. What was she doing? He was young enough to be her son, and she barely knew him. Were the girls who worked at her inn rubbing off on her? Though, to be fair, she was a grown woman and her late husband Nathanael had been gone for a number of years now. Irmina smiled and stood back up. It was time to get back to work. There was always more to do than she had time for. She shivered as her feet touched the back staircase on her way to the inn's kitchen, a vision of her hand on his bare chest flickering through her mind. She was a grown woman and he was old enough—she could do as she pleased. Smiling, she stepped into the large kitchen, catching Emma's glance.

The girl had a knowing and amused look on her sharp-nosed face. "It's like that, is it?"

Irmina resisted the urge to look away and apologize. Instead, she dumped the bandages she was carrying into the basket and went to help with the day's afternoon meal. men were always hungry. She met Emma's eyes as she started to work. "I can do as I please, and yes, that's how it is."

Emma chuckled and smirked, pausing for a brief moment as she put her shoulder against the door to the inn's common room while balancing the tray of food and drink she had. "Aye, a woman's got her needs now and then." With that she left the kitchen, laughing quietly to herself.

Diofrit glanced up from the tray she was loading with a faint smile. "He's a nice man, but I don't think he's staying for very long. He has the look of a man still finding his place."

Irmina looked over at her and replied while pointedly gesturing with the knife she'd been chopping with. "I am not asking him to. There's no rule against me having my fun in the meantime, however." She raised her eyebrows. "You all do that often enough; this one is mine."

They both heard a laugh. Matilda had just come into the kitchen. "I thought that might be what Emma was so amused about. He does have nice hips, even if he will need some time to recover enough for that. Well done, you."

Irmina rolled her eyes and gestured with her knife at the woman while she spoke. "You lot are shameless. A woman should be able to do whatever she wants."

Matilda looked back and grinned slyly as she hoisted a laden tray and left the kitchen. "Oh, you can do whatever you want, but so can we."

As the door swung closed behind the plump woman, it opened again, and Heimeric's large form filled it. He was rehanging his ever-present cudgel back on his belt. "Caught old Theo skulking outside once more. I sent him off." With that the man went back out into the common room. Their inn's strongarm wasn't one for many words.

Irmina sighed. Most of her clientele were older traders, traveling knights and the like, which led to less problems than some other inns had. But she had inherited the Drunken Bear from her late husband, the only way a woman could become a property owner here, and so she needed Heimeric to watch her and the girls' backs. Old Theo, their town drunk, was one reason for this. He tried to steal her mead and wine more than others', because she was a woman.

It was a travesty that her holding on to the inn meant having to hire a man for protection, but Aedonia was what it was, and she wouldn't give up on Nathanael's legacy unless she had to. It was a shame that more men weren't like Edmond. His bare chest flashed to mind; she shivered, then shook it off. Handsome or not, there was work to do and no one else was going to do it for her.

Chapter Twelve: The Drunken Bear

"The common inn is greater than
a king's castle to most Innatraeans."
-Tavid the Traveler

Edmond watched the inn's women weave through the common room, delivering mead and food to guests, while answering questions, taking coins, and fending off unwanted hands. In the days that he'd been at the inn recovering, getting to know these women and their patrons helped him not dwell on thoughts of his grandmother and friends as much. Each of these women had her own personality and flair. Pretty and kind Diofrit with her black curly hair, tall Emma whose tongue was even sharper than her nose, the plump and humorous Matilda, and the very small Mabel who was far cleverer than most. He'd worried about them at first, but most of the inn's guests were peaceful enough, though there seemed to be a few troublemakers who tried to take advantage of the women. But they had Mabel's husband Heimeric. The hulking man was very skilled with his cudgel, as Edmond had seen on a few occasions.

He smiled as Diofrit put a few trenchers loaded with mutton and a flagon of mead on his table. "Thank you!"

She smiled back at him in a friendly manner, pointedly not flirting. "Eat up. You need to get your strength back." With that she started making another round of the room. Her tray bore mutton, sharp cheeses, apples, and crusty bread—standard fare for an inn here.

He'd been here a week or so since the beating he had taken. The women were all very nice to him, but none of them would flirt. All he ever got was normal conversation and the occasional friendly smile. It was as if there was some unspoken rule he was unaware of, one that said because Irmina had taken an interest in him no one else was allowed to even smile in his general direction for a moment longer than necessary.

Not that he minded the situation. It just would have been helpful to have a clearer idea of what was going on; women were all so confusing. He looked over at the inn's main staircase as Irmina made her way down it. She was very attractive and statuesque, with blond hair and those piercing green eyes. She saw him looking and smiled, a smile that said she was busy but welcomed his gaze. It was a smile that hinted at trouble to come.

Edmond laughed at himself and took a pull of mead before diving into his mutton. Still, his mind lingered on Irmina—it was better than dwelling on his grief. He liked her, but he wasn't planning to stay here long, and more pointedly she was old enough to be his mother. As he continued his meal, though, his eyes drifted back to watching her as she moved about the inn's common room. She did this every evening, and in all honesty, he enjoyed watching her. A kind word to travelers here, an admonishment to a local to behave themselves there, keeping an eye on her girls, answering questions, and of course the occasional flirtation—

though never enough to lead a man on. Then suddenly, as she was turning away from a table of rough-looking men, one of them grabbed her arm.

Irmina, not being a timid woman, only took a moment to assess her situation before landing a fierce backhand across his face. He stood up infuriated—his friends laughter not helping the situation. Heimeric headed over immediately, but big as he was there were five of them, and they had weapons. Edmond was on his feet and moving toward the table before he knew it, his hand testing his sword's draw for ease, if needed.

When he arrived, the man already had his hand on the sword at his waist and was speaking angrily. "Are you looking for trouble, big man? You should leave while you can and let us have our fun." The other men at the table, sensing a fight was coming, started to stand up, also laying hands on their sword hilts.

The incident in the alley when he'd first come to town flashed across Edmond's mind. Trying to engage without his weapon had been a bad idea then and would probably be a worse one now. He very purposely placed his hand on his sword's hilt, ready. "Leave now—this isn't your place, and we don't want any trouble."

Heimeric simply nodded, brandishing his cudgel, locking eyes with the man. From what Edmond had seen, the strongarm didn't talk much and liked to either end fights quickly or stop them from happening entirely. Edmond looked over at Irmina and saw her step away. She was a smart woman and could tell where this was headed; thankfully, the men seemed to be ignoring her completely now, since their attention was focused on him and Heimeric.

Edmond owed Irmina a lot for her help, and he didn't want to drag this out. A fight that might damage her inn or hurt people had to end quickly. Heimeric seemed to have the same inclination, because as the man who had grabbed Irmina drew his sword, they both moved in together. Edmond drew and went for the man who had his sword out already, while kicking one of the chairs into another one of the men.

Most fights were over quickly, and this one was no exception; thankfully, it was the exact outcome he'd been hoping for. The other man's sword shattered in twain against Edmond's blade, as the chair he'd kicked made the other man fall to one knee. Heimeric bludgeoned a third of them with his cudgel. The two of them still standing quickly raised their hands, indicating that they no longer had a desire to fight, while the one on his knees stood up to help his friend that had been bludgeoned. The one who had started the whole thing, however, looked around, obviously even more angry at the loss of his sword.

But the other two grabbed him and began dragging him to the inn's front door. "Move, Erik, this ain't worth it, we'll go stay somewhere else."

With that the five of them were gone and then the hush that had settled over the common room was banished by Irmina clapping her hands sharply.

"Heimeric, go see that they do not come back. Girls clean this mess up. Everyone else back to your evenings, the fighting is over, and our bard will be here shortly." Then she looked at Edmond, and he had to remind himself to breathe. The look was thankful, while also being angry, and there was something else there in her green eyes—a smoldering need.

· · · · · ·

Irmina stopped outside Edmond's door—well it was her door, really—thinking. The entire inn was hers, and he was just staying there. In the beginning she had gone in and out of this room with no preamble whatsoever, but he had needed her to bandage and clean his wounds. Now, he was nearly healed and things had changed. Did he want her in the same way? She almost laughed at herself, confused over a man like she was a young girl again. But it was a nice feeling, and she had made her decision. It was time to roll the dice, as some of her patrons would say. Irmina opened the door and stepped inside, trying to look confident. Running an inn was one thing, but her personal needs were another; it had been a long time.

Edmond turned around as she entered. He was standing by the bed and just taking off his shirt. His muscles caught the lamplight, and glowed subtly, as he smiled. "Irmina? I'm doing a lot better. You don't have to tend to me anymore." Her gaze sharpened at his words, and he seemed to grasp that he had said something wrong. He changed the tone of his voice. "Did you want something else?"

She walked up close to him and looked into his eyes, the air between them seeming to heat. The time for second guessing herself was gone. She put one of her hands on his chest. Irmina hoped that the nervousness she felt didn't show in her eyes too much. Her Nathanael had been gone a long while now, and it was time. "Do you not feel it too?"

His eyes softened, and he didn't back away or look surprised. Deep inside their blue depths was something else too, the thing she had hoped for—primal need. "Of course I do, but I'm leaving soon. It wouldn't be right to ask that of you and then disappear."

Irmina let out a tighter, more nervous chuckle than she had intended. He was still so young. Her hand slid down his chest, along his muscles, and grabbed ahold of his breeches, pulling him just a little closer. There was a fleeting beat of tense nervousness, and then she put her other hand on his chin before kissing him.

He was still for a moment, surprised, and then his lips softened against hers and his hands went around her waist.

When they parted slightly, she looked into his eyes again. "I'm not asking you to stay—I'm not leaving either. But while you're here, I want this. It's alright."

He nodded and leaned into her again, his hands and lips both becoming more insistent. This time the kiss was longer, and they both gasped when they parted. Edmond's breath caught as he gazed into her eyes, uncertain about something. "I haven't before."

Irmina found that surprising given how attractive he was, but he was young and still possessed that hesitant naivety. For some reason taking that from him intrigued her. She smiled, only a touch wickedly, before putting one of her hands between his legs, grasping him. "It is not difficult, Edmond—just follow me." He smiled too, less nervous though a bit surprised, probably at her forthrightness. Irmina turned around. "Take my dress off." His hands went to her back immediately. "Gently, I like this one."

He was a little clumsy at first, but listened to her and slowed down, figuring it out relatively quickly. Edmond didn't speak, busy as he was focusing on her body and what he was about to do. The anticipation felt good. Interestingly, he didn't let her dress fall to the ground, but instead eased it down in his hands and knelt, bringing it down gently and allowing her to step out of it. He looked up at her and their eyes met. "You said that you liked this one."

She smiled as he walked over to the room's chair and carefully laid her dress across it. Then he turned around and looked at her. She motioned one of her fingers in a come-hither way. "Come here, Edmond."

He came to stand by her again, obviously admiring her body, even though she still had her chemise on. That would be addressed shortly. Irmina put one of her hands on his chest again and smiled. She could feel his heart quickly beating. Irmina spread her fingers wide, enjoying the feel of his muscles. Her breath quickened, and she firmly shoved him onto the bed, before climbing on top of him. It was time.

Chapter Thirteen:
Nid Yw'r Lle Hwn yn Gartref
(This Place isn't Home)

"Gwrandewch ar y goedwig. Y gwynt trwy gangau'n crychni,
Y dail dan dy draed; maen nhw'n gwybod ble
mae dy galon yn perthyn mewn gwirionedd.
Listen to the forest. The wind through creaking branches, the leaves
under your feet; they know where your heart truly belongs."
-Old Cathyoran Saying

Edmond glanced at Irmina, asleep in her larger bed where he now stayed most nights. He turned toward the window and moved the curtain aside to look out at the town. It was already bustling, even though it was just after sunrise. Ship crews were busy on the docks. Apparently there used to be a ferry here, which is where the town got its name, but the river trade had brought larger ships and with that the ferry had disappeared.

Edmond closed his eyes to listen; he loved the sounds of Innatraeans busily going about their day. Wagons and carts creaked, horses snorted, people shouted or spoke; it all wove a lively clamor he cherished. It also made him dwell less on the departure from his friends and loss of his grandmother. Irmina helped with that too; it was easy to forget past sorrows in the arms of a beautiful woman.

Her hands wrapped around him from behind and she leaned her head on his shoulder. It had been another few weeks since they'd first started sleeping together, and truthfully, he'd stayed longer in Talberston's Crossing than he'd meant to because of her. She said their time together was a casual, fleeting thing, and that it was okay for him to go, but he didn't like the idea. Truthfully, being with her kept his mind on the present and gave him joy. Things like relationships were different back home in Aliselle Falls; this was easier even though it bothered him a bit. He eased the curtain back into place.

"Good morning." He could feel her lips smiling as she kissed his neck and her hands traveled down his bare chest to his hips. "You're listening to the town again."

"The people. I love the sounds of normal everyday Innatraeans going about their lives."

She bit his ear gently. "You will love Bethseda even more. There are thousands more people and sounds there."

Edmond sighed heavily. His shoulders slumped. She always said those things so casually—the ones that meant he was leaving. She was right, though, he would probably like the capital even more, and he knew his time to leave was coming. Edmond loved towns and people, but he had also grown up in the woods. The sounds of forests and animals were something he enjoyed too. Since he'd mostly recovered, Edmond had started taking short walks in the nearby woods for exercise and the feeling of home. Something in those sounds had changed recently though, as if even they knew he didn't really belong here. This place wasn't his home, much as he liked the town and Irmina.

"You always say that so easily, but you're right. I like it here, stayed longer for you, but this place doesn't feel like home—not really."

Her fingers stilled at the cord holding up his breeches, and she laughed softly. "You are always so serious when you've been thinking too much. I know this place isn't where you belong, and I never asked you to stay longer." Her hand reached into his breeches and took hold of him. "It's okay to enjoy moments of pleasure and happiness. You're still young. Relax and let some of that weight off your shoulders."

Wasn't that what good men were supposed to do? Think about important things in their lives and do the right thing? But what if the right thing was contrary to a person's thinking? Nothing in what Edmond had learned from his family and friends back home had taught him how to deal with these situations. Then again, he knew that Talberston's Crossing wasn't his destiny, so wasn't it better that she was at peace with him moving on? She even encouraged it. Edmond's thoughts must have shown on his face, because Irmina laughed again before grabbing his now undone breeches and pulling him back toward the bed. "You're truly alright with me leaving?"

Irmina laughed for a third time. He liked the sound more than he'd be willing to admit, or maybe he had just gotten used to it. Either way he would miss his time here with her. "Edmond, you were never meant to stay here, and I knew that from the beginning." Her hands seized his breeches. "Now take these off and come say goodbye to me the right way before you go."

Petra shrieked in terror, though no sound seemed to escape her lips. Her entire being convulsed in loss and pain. The man laughed, dropping her mother's body and turning toward her father. Petra tried to claw her way out, tried to escape, tried to run, tried to do anything. But these men—Jhorians—were bigger and stronger than her. Her face ended up in the mud, her eyes locked with the now colorless dead eyes of her mother. There was no hope.

Why was this happening? Her mind grasped for escape, for anything to dull the pain. Anything that would give her a safe place to go, somewhere to avoid it all, to not think about what was happening and what she had lost.

The brutal Jhorians had been here for days now, but it seemed like longer. Questioning their family, their farmhands, and their friends. Asking them who else could Weave and eventually killing everyone because no one could tell them anything. Her uncle had tried to lie and was strung up for the crows; the same fate had befallen anyone who resisted or said something these men didn't like. The women and girls got the worst of it; even thinking about what had happened to her cousin Claudia made Petra want to retch. She had been spared so far because her safety was leverage the men could use.

"Who else, old man? Answer us now or you'll watch what happens to your little girl."

Her father was silent, his eyes flashing between anger and fear, mouth working silently. What could you say in the face of such unrestrained hatred and violence? His body fell next to her mother's as Petra screamed, feeling more like an animal than an Innatraean. Her face was shoved into the mud, where she instinctively closed her eyes. She couldn't weep or scream without swallowing mud and farmyard refuse. It would be a grim end—one she almost welcomed, if it meant this would be over.

Her brother. That's why this was happening. Because he could Weave, and they'd seen him. A family member being able to wield magic was enough reason for the Jhorians to condone destroying them and taking everything they had. The bastards called it the Will of Jhoras. No god who demanded this was worthy of faith. The man holding Petra pulled her face out of the mud, trying to make her look at her dead parents. She refused. She kept her eyes closed and he hit her, a blow to her side that sent sharp pain throughout her body.

"Look or he's next."

Her twin brother. Leonhard. He could Weave. He had been showing her the only trick he knew, a little flash of light. Such a small thing, nothing really. She had laughed, like always, finding joy in who her dear brother was. But this time they had seen, and now the great holy church had come for her family. Petra opened her eyes, slowly and with more pain than she had ever known, but she couldn't lose him too. Not now. She prayed inside of her mind, to anyone listening.

The white-clad men sneered and laughed as the one whose tabard was now stained with her parents' blood wiped his knife on a red-stained rag and sheathed it. "That's a good girl. Now we'll let your brother live, at least until the Inquisitor arrives." They laughed again. How could any faith encourage such cruelty?

Leonhard couldn't see this, and the small part of her that was still able to think was thankful for that; he had always been softer. She looked at him. He was gagged and bound next to her, but the man holding Petra yanked her backwards painfully. "None of that now, little girl. He can't see or hear you. Wouldn't want him Weaving, might have to kill him then." The others laughed and he pulled her hair, dragging her onto her back and away from the others. "You, however? It's time for us to hear you scream."

Petra realized what the man meant and what he intended for her. She screamed again, summoning the very last of her strength and tried to fight. But she couldn't do anything. She was bound, exhausted, hurt, and he was easily twice her size. Her flailing might as well have been that of a little child.

He dragged her behind one of the barns and laughed before crouching down next to her. "Now, I'm going to cut your hands loose. It's easier for me that way. If you fight me, I'll do more than just take you." His knife slid between her arms and cut the rope holding her wrists and hands. Then the man laughed as he grabbed a hold of her and rolled her over.

Petra closed her eyes. There was nothing she could do, and even this wasn't the worst of it. Her parents were murdered and an Inquisitor was coming for her brother. What else could they take from her? There was nothing left, not anymore.

Then she heard a voice inside of her. A vast and unyielding force within her that demanded the attention of her very soul. "Fight, child of Cathyor. So long as you draw breath and your heart beats, there is hope. Rise."

Petra felt it pulse inside of her and strength flowed through her veins, sighing into her limbs. Her soul screamed. This wasn't life. She was more than this. There was a power deep inside of her. Something hidden, eons old, that demanded she listen. Petra opened her eyes, and with a clenched jaw, she moved.

Petra shouldn't have been able to. She was broken and the man was bigger than her, but she took the knife from him as he leaned over her and shoved the cruel blade deep into his throat. In that moment, they stared at one another as he bled out. His eyes were shocked, and his blood was warm as it flowed out of him and onto her. She didn't know blood could be that warm. A part of her briefly thought she should be scared. She had killed a man. Taken his life. Even though they had killed her parents, taken her brother, and tried to do worse, it should have felt wrong. But taking this man's life felt right. It felt like justice.

"Rise, child of Cathyor, you must go now, they will come for you. Run. Listen to the forest."

Petra could hear the other men shouting rude jokes and laughing on the other side of the barn. If they found their dead companion while she was still here, then what would follow would be worse than death. She grunted and pushed the man's body aside, then rolled onto her stomach and got to her feet. "Listen to the forest." She could feel something in the wind, like a whisper beyond her hearing, calling her into its embrace, into the forest.

Petra ran for her life into the darkening forest and night. I will come back for you, Leonhard, I promise, somehow.

Chapter Fourteen: Petra

"Mae'r bywyd hwn yn perthyn i'r dewr.
This life belongs to the brave."
-Old Cathyoran Saying

"Drop the knife. It is not your blade." Petra could hear the voice better now, as if it had gotten stronger. It sounded like the whisper of leaves in a sacred grove, ancient and alive. She dropped the bloodied knife at the voice's command. She wasn't sure if that voice inside her head was her soul, a Weaver, a deity whose name she didn't know, or something else entirely. But it had given her strength when she needed it, a pathway to escape despair, and more importantly, hope. So, she dropped the knife and ran deeper into the dark forest and night.

Petra wanted to rescue her brother and vowed she would, but there were too many Jhorians. Worse, from the sounds of yelling and the light of torches behind her, she assumed they had found their man, the one she had killed, the one who had been trying to rape her. These men were animals—no, demons—and she wanted to kill them all. But there were too many and she needed to survive. Her vengeance needed to live on. *I'll come back for you, Leonhard, stay strong.*

The sounds of shouting echoed through the night, drawing closer, and the thunder of approaching horses told her there was no way out. They were faster than her and there were so many of them. But Leonhard needed her—there was no one else, and to rescue him she had to survive first. She took a deep breath and ran, giving everything she had left in this world. The lilting feminine voice spoke to her again. "Take the cloak. Hide. Hood yourself. Now!"

A cloak hung ahead, its tree-and-sword symbol shimmering with faint power against the dark night. Petra snatched it without pause and threw it over her shoulders. "Be brave, child of Cathyor. Ahead of you, follow the glimmers. Hide and wrap yourself in the cloak." Did the lilting voice, woven with creaking branches, rise from the forest itself?

A small glimmer of light flashed in front of her, and she ran toward it, out of breath, her pulse thundering. The voice spoke softly, almost soothing, like a warm breeze. "Be quiet. Still." Petra dove to the ground and wrapped herself in the cloak. It hummed faintly against her skin, its fabric pulsing with unnatural warmth. She took a deep breath and held it, quiet and still. Her heart pounded too loudly; she was sure they would hear it.

A group of Jhorians on horseback came near. She could see their torchlight through the cloak's thin protection. Petra closed her eyes and prayed to whatever voice she was hearing inside her head. "Please, I want to live!"

"She isn't here. You're sure she ran this way?"

"I saw her! She can't be far."

"Alright, men! Spread out and search the whole forest if you must! Find that godless witch and bring me her head!"

The men moved on, spreading out into the forest, hunting and shouting. Their white Jhorian tabards and armor gleamed in their torchlight. A fearful flame indeed, if they found her.

Petra opened her eyes, stunned, and breathed out, watching them ride away from her into the dark night. She didn't understand. They must have stared straight through her. She'd felt their torchlight brush the cloak, but they hadn't seen her. "Be brave, child of Cathyor. I am with you. Stand. Follow the glimmers, go quickly!"

Petra stood, banishing her confusion, and ran toward the flash of light she had just seen. It faded as she leaned against a tall tree nearby where the glimmer had been, exhausted. How was she going to survive this night? Was the voice enough? The desperate need to survive fought against the desire to kill them all and save her brother. There was no way she could do this alone, but who else was there?

The horses were nearing. She leaned into the tree and wrapped the cloak around herself, closing her eyes. Their torchlight came and went, moving quickly with the dreaded pounding of their horses' hooves. They didn't see her. The cloak must be magic. But from where? "Follow the glimmers, child of Cathyor."

Petra raised her head, gazing into the silent dark around her. A cold wind swept through the trees. Its chill sharpened her senses. An owl hooted in the dark, and she saw another flash ahead. Petra ran toward that brief light. I will survive. I will come back for you, Leonhard, and I will kill them all for what they did to us.

· · · · · ·

Caleb stepped onto the farmhouse's porch and looked out into the night. He didn't like having to stay here; this farm belonged to a family of sinners. He wanted to burn it down and take their damned witch son north to Porto de la Luce. But the girl had killed one of his men and fled into the forest. His body and hands tensed at the thought: One of his men was murdered by the godless witch's vile twin sister. They would find the wretch and make her scream before the end. They would leave no witnesses to question the Will of Jhoras.

Caleb reached his hand down and touched the cloth he kept tucked into his belt—the one stained with the blood of every sinner he'd taken during his time serving the Holy Church of Jhoras. Its stained contours, a reminder of his holy work, steadied him. It calmed his nerves and helped him focus. There was once a time when such things disturbed his sense of morality. He had questioned the acts required of him and his companions in the name of Jhoras, because they had seemed like sin. Caleb still remembered his first sinner. He had hesitated then, unsure of his right to take the life of another. That mistake had let a godless witch kill two anointed brethren, forging his ruthless path. Now he understood the need for those who could do what was necessary, he understood the need for brave and pious men to bring the Will of Jhoras into the darkness.

He wanted to add the witch girl's blood to the cloth for what she had done. Murderers received no mercy; justice and the Will of Jhoras demanded it.

Then one of the distant torchlights started approaching the farmhouse, and Edriel materialized out of the darkness. The man was a good soldier, if a bit on the unimaginative side. He saluted Caleb before speaking. "Commander, the hunters have not come back yet. Do you want us to go look for them or secure the farm for the night?"

The current situation was incredibly frustrating, though not worrisome. The girl had gotten lucky grabbing Ethan's knife and stabbing him in the throat, but the man had never been a cautious one and had stupidly cut the girl loose. She was proving resourceful in avoiding capture, but the dark forest's many hiding places hindered them. She was not a trained warrior and there had been no evidence of her being able to Weave like her witch of a brother. "Secure the farm and set up rotating patrols. The men will need rest."

Caleb forced himself to stand erect and crossed his arms behind his back while watching Edriel retreat into the darkness to issue his orders. Caleb was exhausted. The search had stretched into the long night hours, but commanders in the Fist of Jhoras were not allowed to show weakness. After Edriel was gone, Caleb sighed and retreated into the farmhouse.

The farmhouse, an austere structure with few decorations or furniture, held little beyond necessity. He sat at the crude table and looked down at the godless witch lying bound and gagged on the floor, with the cloth Catena wrapped around his eyes and ears. The Catena, or "witch's chain," shrouded captives' sight and hearing, blocking their ability to Weave. The godless witch was crying again, as if this wasn't all his fault for being born a sinner.

Caleb took the stained and chipped glass he'd found earlier and poured himself a finger of the cheap brandy that had once belonged to the family who had lived here. Alcohol was a sin, so Caleb would have to confess upon returning home. His wife was a Daughter of Jhoras; it was her duty to listen. He put the glass down and sighed, closing his eyes, feeling the brandy burn his throat. Then the witch started crying louder, so Caleb kicked him. "Quiet, godless witch, your time of judgment is coming."

It was true, he had received the message earlier today. Inquisitor Durand would finally be headed in their direction in a few days. There had been an event in Haversfjord that required a lengthy investigation. In fact, Caleb and his men had initially been dispatched south to help the Inquisitor, but then one of his scouts had seen the godless witch Weaving. Caleb kicked the witch again, his righteous judgment craving the wretch's blood for his cloth. It was, after all, his fault that Caleb was stuck on this godless farm, and that his wretch of a sister had killed Ethan. But as Fist of Jhoras, their duty was to stop and investigate Weaving wherever found, and take the godless into custody for questioning, leaving them no choice.

Caleb poured himself another finger of the brandy. His only concern was failing to capture the girl before Inquisitor Durand arrived. The man would already be irritable, and that would unleash disaster. In truth, it was but a mere worry. She was a farm girl, and his men were seasoned anointed. They would capture the godless wretch before Inquisitor Durand arrived. Then Caleb would make her bleed for Ethan's death, adding her blood to his stained cloth.

CHAPTER FIFTEEN:

ARWRIAETH

(HEROISM)

Petra leaned against a tree trunk, gasping for breath, her lungs burning and her heart beating so fast she feared it would break through her chest. But she couldn't stop—those demons who called themselves Jhorians were still chasing her. So far, she had only managed to stay ahead of them because of the voice she'd been hearing inside her head, the flashes of light guiding her, and the even stranger magical cloak that made her invisible. "Where am I going?" A few hours earlier, Petra had discovered that she could talk to the voice, that whatever it was could hear her and would usually reply.

"Keep going, child of Cathyor. There is hope in the forest, his blood sings. Find him."

Another flash of light appeared far ahead, Petra pushed herself off the tree and started running again, almost stumbling from exhaustion. They would catch her soon if she didn't find somewhere safe to hide. "What do you mean his blood sings? Who is he? Where are you leading me?"

Horse hooves echoed behind her; they sounded like death thumping a dirge meant for her alone. "Mae gwaed arwyr yn canu."

What language was that? The voice had never used such strange words before, and Petra had no idea what they meant. But there wasn't much of a choice given her other options. Another flash of light came from her left, and it sent Petra darting, but her foot caught on a root and she fell. The horses' hooves were closer now. She could almost feel their torches' searing glow on her back. "Down the hill, there is no choice, they almost have you. Hurry, child of Cathyor. Run!"

Petra's skin prickled as torchlight shone on her. She pushed herself up into a stumbling run toward the steep hill ahead. One of their voices boomed through the night as she dove down the slope, heedless of all but escape. The voice felt like doom. "There she is! Seize the godless witch!"

The demonic Jhorians and their horses came to the top of the slope as Petra rolled down the steep incline. "She's not going to make it out of that, let's go around and grab whatever's left of her at the bottom."

In a moment of clarity, Petra knew the man was right. She was rolling down a steep slope in the dark night—one wrong hit and she would break, but at least it wouldn't be in the cruel hands of those men and their cursed faith. "I will protect you, child of Cathyor. Shelter in my hands." She must have been delirious with exhaustion, grief, and pain. Two giant hands rose from the ground, wrapping around her.

A strange warmth enveloped Petra as the night stilled, the brutal fall slowing until she gently rolled down the hill. Then a wind blew over her, bringing with it the loud creak of tree branches. Petra rolled onto a wide-open path, and felt something pick her up before placing her on her feet. "Ahead of you, the campfire. He's there. Run, child of Cathyor!"

Petra ran, putting everything she had left into moving her legs and screamed, "Help me!"

As she ran, their torchlight lit the other end of the path. "There she is! She made it through the fall, grab her!" The horses started coming toward her quickly, and Petra swore she could hear them drawing their swords. Terror gripped her heart, and her breath hitched—she feared they would take her. "Please, I don't want to die!"

A man by the campfire stood to look in her direction. Then a sword floated into the air beside him, strange symbols blazing along its blade. In that moment of shock, Petra tripped over something and fell onto her face. The night disappeared as she blacked out, but she thought the man ran past her toward the Jhorians. "Save me, please…"

. . . . . .

Edmond stared into the wavering campfire at the rabbit he'd snared earlier. It was taking too long to cook, and he was hungry. That wasn't really where his mind was, though. He was thinking about how nice it would have been to be lying in Irmina's warm bed, instead of being out in the woods by himself—thoughts of which were interrupted by the sound of a loud wind, but nothing around him stirred. Curious, he looked around the small clearing where he'd made camp and at the nearby trail, though he couldn't see very far in the dark. Tree branches creaked loudly, yet he couldn't feel a breeze in his hair. Confused, he squinted into the dark night. Suddenly, there were riders coming, galloping toward him with torches. Jhorians. Their white tabards and steel armor gleamed in the torchlight like beacons, stark against the blood-red three-quartered crosses on their chests.

A girl's voice screamed. "Help me!"

One of them yelled. "There she is! She made it through the fall, grab her!"

Was she running from them toward his camp? Edmond stood up, suddenly feeling like his night was going to be much more exciting and less lonely than expected.

There were only a few reasons Jhorians would be chasing a lone girl, and Edmond didn't agree with a single one of them. He stepped forward and stopped for a moment in shock as a voice seemed to speak inside his head. "Cian, protect her."

It was a voice Edmond thought he recognized from long ago, a voice he somehow knew. "Mother...?" Why was she calling him Cian?

The night seemed to slow down to individual heartbeats, as his sword floated out of its scabbard in front of him, the strange writing he'd glimpsed in Haversfjord flared along the blade as it hung before him. Edmond started to step back in shock, but the voice came into his head again. "Cian, wield your sword, protect her. These men's fates belong to your blade. Take them."

Edmond put his hand out and the sword snapped into his grip as he rushed forward to engage the Jhorians.

"Please, I don't want to die!" The girl tripped and fell as he ran past her, but he didn't have time to help her up. The men were on him. There were four of them, all in armor and on horseback, with swords. He had no chance, but he couldn't let them take the girl. He didn't know her, but he knew that voice, and his sword had been his father's. Sometimes you had to embrace who you were and face the consequences later.

The Jhorians came for him, expecting to ride him down and slice him into pieces with their swords—as Edmond did too. But the glowing light from his sword's writing seemed to bleed like a liquid, tracing the blade and streaking into the air as he moved. The light tore through all it touched like a frail cloth. Blades shattered, armor and flesh broke open in violent sprays of warm blood, and torches fell onto their now screaming horses. As the men and their mounts toppled to the ground, the night seemed to return to normal speed, the beating of his own heart quieted, and he was left facing one last enemy.

The man's white and steel adornments gleamed in the firelight and his eyes were grim. The man had dropped his torch, no longer needing it amid the blazing corpses of his companions and their horses. The charnel smell of burning flesh filled Edmond's nostrils as the man lifted his long sword, now holding it in both hands, looking at Edmond menacingly. The man's face said he was confronting what he believed to be an evil demon. "Who are you? What are you?" The man stepped to his left, over the bodiless flaming arm of one of the dead men. Edmond shifted his feet, mirroring the man's movement, and remained quiet. "Sinner." He raised his sword higher. "Demon." He lunged for Edmond, striking out with his sword. "Witch!"

Edmond stepped back quickly, avoiding the strike. He thought enough had died tonight. The man was clearly an experienced fighter; the others probably had been too. He wasn't sure what had happened or how his sword unleashed such ruin. "Leave now and you can live."

The man screamed at Edmond, his eyes gleaming with madness, spittle spraying from his mouth. "I am Ser Gideon Ludheim and I will end you, witch!" He lunged for Edmond again, a streak of maddened white and gleaming steel slicing through the air.

Edmond moved to engage Gideon. He had offered him the chance to leave, but hatred had overcome his reason. "Very well, Gideon. I'm sorry."

Perhaps Edmond had overestimated himself—or underestimated the man's skill as a warrior—for the engagement went wrong almost immediately. Their blades met, and as Gideon's blade shattered, he twisted aside. Gideon's shoulder hit him in the chest, and he kicked Edmond's legs out from under him as their swords flew aside. "Now it's time to die, witch!" The man drew a vicious looking knife and dove on top of Edmond as his back hit the dirt.

The move startled Edmond, and he barely managed to shove the knife aside. Its blade cut along his right cheek before being shoved into the ground next to his face by the other man's momentum. Warm blood streaked along Edmond's cheek, now throbbing with pain, and dripping down his neck as he struggled for control of the knife.

As they fought, Edmond couldn't help but recall something Marged had told him once: "In war there is no mercy, kill your enemy or die.

His opponent pulled the knife back up and leaned in again, trying to stab Edmond. It was like fighting a rabid animal. Their legs kneed or pinned one another. They rolled beside a horse's burning corpse, and Edmond's shoulder grazed the flames. He screamed in pain. Gideon seized the moment, attempting to force his knife into Edmond's flesh.

"Focus, Cian!" came the voice.

Edmond forced himself to ignore the pain and rolled even closer to the fire with all his strength, heaving Gideon into the perilous flames. The man screamed, and Edmond took the knife and stabbed him as the flames greedily consumed his body.

Edmond lay there panting, trying to catch his breath, listening to the sound of crackling fire around him. Once his breathing normalized, he rolled over onto all fours and surveyed the area quickly. One of the horses was still twitching, but all the Jhorians were dead. He saw his sword lying near his shattered opponent's blade and stood up on shaky legs to go get it. His gaze fell upon the girl; she was still lying where she had fallen, so he went to check on her, picking up his sword and putting the horse out of its misery on the way.

Edmond, aching and spent, knelt by her. He set his sword aside, then gently rolled her onto her back to check her breathing. She was brutally battered, bloodied and dirty, but alive. The tree-and-sword emblem on her cloak seemed familiar somehow. She appeared about his age; it was odd, what caught his eye now. What had led her to his camp? He gazed into the still night. What had happened? Eyeing his sword, he wondered if it always harbored such power. The voice! "Mother...?"

"Well done, my son. Keep her safe. I love you."

Chapter Sixteen:
Enaid Dyn
(A Man's Soul)

> *"Mae enaid dyn yn dangos ei hun yng*
> *nghalonnau'r merched o'i gwmpas.*
> *A man's soul shows itself in the*
> *hearts of the women around him."*
> -Old Cathyoran Saying

Elspeth hoisted herself up into Styfnig's saddle and took a hold of his reins. The horse's name meant "Stubborn," and she had named the animal after Archibald, though she would never tell him that. Both man and horse shared the same temperament, though at least the latter listened to her once in a while. She snapped the beast's reins to get it moving and glanced at Archibald. "It's time to go, old man."

On his horse, Glendid, he came up next to her. The animal's name meant "Beauty," and Elspeth had her suspicions about why he'd chosen it; sometimes he was truly endearing. *Sometimes.* "You could show at least a little bit of gratitude. Kidner and I did save your life."

Elspeth sighed and smiled at him, her irritation easing. "I am grateful, my love, truly. But we have to hurry. I was waylaid for weeks, healing. The boy, Edmond—Cian, our prince. He could be in Bethseda by now!"

Archibald grumbled back at her. "He was on foot, and we have horses. We'll catch up to him."

She eyed him sideways. "We have to catch him before he enlists! If he truly is Prince Cian, then he's the key to everything!"

Now he looked annoyed. "I know, we will catch him. But you still need to take it easy.

She rolled her eyes at him. "You fuss over nothing. It has been weeks. I'm fine."

He grumbled again. "Stubborn, reckless woman."

"You worry too much."

"Someone has to."

Elspeth laughed and patted Styfnig; it was a fitting name indeed. They sounded like an old married couple, as good as wed. "That's what I love about you," she said, eyeing him sideways, "old man."

Archibald laughed too. "We make quite the pair, don't we? We'll find him, and Rhiannon willing bring back what was lost." His fists tightened on his horse's reins, his eyes blazing with resolve. "Hopefully along the way we'll make a few of those bastards pay for it, too."

That was one of the reasons she loved him, lack of marriage and stubbornness aside—few men were made like Archibald Stallwood. She nodded without a word. Such things didn't need lengthy discussion; they both knew who the bastards were and what they must answer for. As Haversfjord faded from view behind them, six more riders came out of the trees, joining the two of them on the road. Her army, small as it was, brimmed with true Cathyorans.

Archibald left Kidner back in Haversfjord to look after things. The town was important to him, and it couldn't go for long without a reeve. That meant they were eight. Could eight souls rewrite Cathyor's fate? They had to. Their prince had been found, and it was up to them now. Elspeth's hands tightened on the reins, and she nodded to herself. *I will do this.* She looked around at her companions. *No, we will do this.*

Caoimhe guided her horse close to Elspeth as Archibald pulled back toward the others. "Kidner told us about the boy, Edmond? His actions in Haversfjord were admirable. Do you truly think he's Prince Cian?"

Elspeth nodded. "By Rhiannon, I swear he has to be. What other man could possibly wield a horse head pommel sword that cuts through other men's steel like that?"

Caoimhe nodded in return. "May Rhiannon shed her light and grace upon us. I'm with you, sister." They clasped hands. "Hyd at farwolaeth neu ailenedigaeth." Until death or rebirth.

. . . . . .

Petra's mind plunged into a nightmare. The sun burned black, mirroring the rot in some men's souls. One of the Jhorians dragged her cousin Claudia behind the nearby barn; his pure white tabard and shining steel armor seemed to reflect blackness, and the three-quartered cross on his chest was bleeding. It wasn't long after that Claudia started screaming. Petra looked up from her place on the ground—there was blood everywhere. She laid her head down, not wanting to see any more... Someone shoved her face into the mud... Petra woke, gasping for breath. Her chest heaved. She couldn't get enough air into her aching lungs. She flailed frantically.

"You're safe here, calm down, you'll hurt yourself!"

A man's voice—one she didn't know. A hand touched her shoulder and Petra recoiled in fear. She scrambled backwards away from him, planning to get up and run, but the voice interrupted her panic. "You are safe, child of Cathyor. Be calm. Breathe."

She stopped, breathing rapidly, trying to relax, still fighting her instinctual need to flee. But the voice had kept her safe thus far.

After a few moments, when she could finally breathe normally and felt calmer, Petra took in her surroundings. She was near a campfire and she had been covered with a blanket. She saw the young man sitting across the fire from her. He looked worried and a bit apprehensive. A memory flashed across her mind, of herself running in the night toward a fire and a young man standing up with a magic sword. It was the same man.

He nodded at seeing her calm and smiled encouragingly. "You're safe here, no one's going to hurt you. I promise."

Petra took a deep breath. "You saved me. Thank you." She saw they were alone. He bore a bad-looking gash on his cheek, and his clothes were burned. "Those men, the Jhorians, did they?!" She looked around quickly, scared again.

"They're gone. I took care of them and pulled their bodies into the trees. You're safe." He smiled again, flexing his arm and touching his cheek gently. "There's food there. I'm sure you're hungry. I'm fine, just a little worse for wear."

She looked where he had pointed and saw that there was indeed food—rabbit, bread, and cheese. Her stomach rumbled and she started eating, suddenly feeling ravenous. The last few days had brimmed with hardship and terror. She mumbled "thank you" between stuffing hurried bites of food into her mouth.

He chuckled a little but quickly became serious. "Why were those Jhorians chasing you?"

Petra lowered her bread and cheese, looking down. Fresh tears spilled instantly, and her throat tightened. "They... My family..." She looked at him, feeling despair grip her heart anew. "They killed everyone, except me and my brother. I have to go back for him!"

He put his elbows on his knees and leaned his chin on his closed fist, eyes growing even more serious. "Why?"

"I... My brother... Can..." She didn't know if she could trust him, but she couldn't save Leonhard alone, and the voice had brought her here. There was no other choice.

He spoke, breaking her thoughts. "Your brother, can he Weave?"

Petra's eyes widened. "How...?!"

He relaxed a little, and leaned back, like he had figured things out and knew exactly what to say now. "My name is Edmond. I grew up around a friend who could Weave, so I guessed." He looked at the fire. "There are few reasons Jhorians pursue Weavers." He looked up again and their eyes met. "I am very sorry about your family, but I'll help you save your brother."

"I'm Petra. Yes, my brother, Leonhard, can Weave." She shuddered and felt more tears streaming down her face. "They saw him Weave and then killed everyone." She leaned over, racked by sobs.

A few moments later his hand rested on her shoulder. "Your brother, he's still alive?"

She tried to answer him between sobs; some small part of her hoped this stranger would really help save her brother. "Yes..."

Edmond slowly sat down near her. "Take your time. When you're ready, we will make a plan." He sighed audibly. "Jonaas and Rosalie would kill me if I left a Weaver in Jhorian hands." He went silent for a moment, as Petra's tears slowed. "I could never forgive myself for something like that."

He was going to help her. The voice had led her to him, and he was going to help her save Leonhard. Something inside Petra gave way, like a shadowed veil holding her hope and trust at bay. She slowly laid her head down on Edmond's shoulder and started weeping again. "Thank you."

He didn't speak; he just gently put his hands around her and waited, showing a patience and reticence she didn't know a man could have—not after what she'd seen. Eventually, Petra quieted and just lay there, breathing, feeling safe for the first time in what seemed like forever. "We'll need a plan when you're ready." He paused, squeezing her shoulder. "I know you're hurt and tired, but we don't have long if we're going to save him."

Petra sat up with determination. She had to save Leonhard; there was nothing else that mattered now. "Yes, we have to save him. He's the only person I have left!"

Edmond nodded. "How many Jhorians are still there? Is there an Inquisitor?"

Petra closed her eyes, trying to picture her family's farm, while keeping her grief away. "There are six of those bastards left, and no Inquisitor." Images of the previous night flashed across her mind. Four had chased her, and Edmond said he had killed them. She opened her eyes and looked at him, hope and awe warring with the despair inside of her. "You killed all four last night, didn't you? Your sword! Who are you?"

He sighed heavily. "I honestly don't know, aside from the name I was given and where I grew up." He looked into the fire. "Yes, my sword has magic powers, but I don't know where from or why." He closed his eyes. "My family lineage—everything—has been brought into question recently." Edmond opened his eyes and looked at her, determined. "But you can trust me, and I'm going to help you. Together we'll rescue your brother, I promise." He picked up a nearby stone and laid it on the ground between them. "Gather objects and use them to show me the layout of your home. We need to plan."

She watched him as he spoke—trepidation and hope, trust and darkness, all warring within her now-fragile heart. "Trust him, child of Cathyor. Save your brother. The roots of destiny bloom within you both. Embrace them. Grow."

Petra picked up a small stick shaped like one of their barns and placed it near the stone he'd set. "Alright, there's a barn right here."

Chapter Seventeen: The Geisterschwert Family Farm

*"Mae tynged yn pwyso ei hun yng nghalon pob arwr.
Destiny weighs itself in every hero's heart."*
-Old Cathyoran Saying

Petra closed her eyes and took a deep breath, remembering Edmond's words from the day before. "In war, the appearance of vulnerability can sometimes lure your enemy into making a fatal mistake." She opened her eyes, feeling stronger, and took her last few steps out of the trees, onto the open road that led to her family's farm. She stepped into the middle of the road and stared at her family's home, fighting the terror of what she knew had happened there. "With only six men, their patrols are spread out. If we can catch even one of them away from the others, it will give us a better chance of success." She looked at the distant lone Jhorian on horseback, down the road from her, trying to look confident and defiant. More courageous than scared and sad. The man immediately turned his horse around and started galloping toward her. Petra steeled herself. It was time. Their plan had begun, and it was her brother Leonhard's only hope.

The hoof beats echoed her beating heart, a thumping of both hope and terror. Petra breathed deeply and waited. When he was nearly halfway toward her, she felt her face take on a look of utter fear, before bolting back toward the trees. The Jhorian followed her. She knew he would; he believed it was his job to punish her for being the sister of a godless witch. The horse's hooves became louder. She was almost there, but he almost had her too. Was Edmond waiting as he said? Could she trust him as much as she hoped? *Please.*

She broke into the trees and ran past Edmond, who was behind a tree on her left. Moments later, the Jhorian was there, his sneer of hatred burned into her. Petra no longer had to feign her terror. The horse screamed and the man shouted, but then came the sickening sound of rending flesh and tearing metal—and afterward, only silence. Petra almost fell as she leaned against a tree before glancing back. Edmond was there and her pursuer lay in bloodied, torn steel-covered pieces on the forest floor. The glowing sword's light dimmed as she closed her eyes. *Thank you.*

"You have done well, child of Cathyor. Rescue your brother, prove your heart." Petra's eyes shot open. Prove her heart? The voice had never said anything like that before. What did it mean?

Edmond cleaned his sword's blade on the dead man's tabard, sheathed it, and walked over to her. "Are you alright?"

She nodded. "I am, thank you for being where you said you'd be. I owe you so much."

"You don't owe me anything. Men like these deserve justice, and I gave you my word."

Petra smiled in spite of herself and everything going on. "Most men's words are not worth the mud on their boots. You're a good man, Edmond."

He nodded and smiled, then his face grew serious. "You said there was a game trail not far from here, that loops around the other side of the farm?"

Petra nodded and pushed herself up from the tree. "Yes, it's this way."

Edmond immediately started walking toward where she indicated. "Come on, we need to keep moving. Surprise is our only advantage."

Petra followed him. She kept quiet, even though she wanted to say that it wasn't their only advantage. Edmond's advanced fighting skills and his magic sword counted too. She didn't know how to voice her thoughts yet—too much was happening. What had the voice meant by telling her to prove her heart? She couldn't help but remember something the voice had said yesterday. "Trust him, child of Cathyor. Save your brother. The roots of destiny bloom within you both. Embrace them. Grow." Who was Edmond really? What destiny awaited them? Petra didn't know, and truthfully, for now, all that mattered was saving Leonhard.

. . . . . .

Edmond carefully stepped around the dead Jhorian's corpse, this one had come for them on foot; the patrols didn't use horses so near to the farm. Petra lured the man by throwing small stones at him and yelling obscenities. The Jhorian had died on his knees, vehemently screaming that she was a sinner and godless wretch. Now the man's body lay by the game trail to be eaten by wild animals—a kinder fate than he deserved. Edmond leaned on a nearby tree to get a better look at the farmyard. He was worried that the noise may have drawn the attention of the other Jhorians.

Edmond had been right to worry. The Jhorians had heard, but they weren't heading this way; instead, they were forming a defensive perimeter around the main farmhouse. It made sense—five of their men were missing and they'd just heard a sixth screaming before he went quiet. They were being cautious. Edmond had no idea how he and Petra achieved so much with so little harm. Maybe it was luck, his sword's newfound abilities, or his mother's spirit. Hearing her voice still bothered him, but he didn't have time to dwell on that right now. More than likely, it was the training he had received from Marged and Jonathan back home; both were highly skilled former warriors. He sighed and looked at Petra. She was exhausted, but holding up well, all things considered. "They're going on the defensive. We'll need to rethink our plan." He rubbed his chin, thinking, as she came to look too.

"Can we still save my brother?" Her voice sounded scared.

He nodded. "Yes, we can, we are just going to have to do it a different way than we planned."

She nodded, obviously trying to stay strong. "What do we need to do?"

"You said that there are game trails all around the farm?"

"Yes!"

"Okay, this will be difficult, but I think it's our best chance. I am going to approach the men outside in the open and engage them. It doesn't look like they have any archers." He looked at the Jhorians one more time to verify what he was saying, then his eyes met Petra's. "You'll need to sneak around to the other side of the farmhouse and get your brother free. I'm assuming they have him tied up inside, since no other buildings are being guarded and I don't see an Inquisitor yet. Signal me if you can. I'll hold them off."

Petra nodded. She still looked scared, but there was bravery deep in her brown eyes, too. "I can do it!"

Edmond nodded and walked back over to the Jhorian's corpse. All of them carried the same wicked knives as well as their swords. He took it and held it out toward Petra. "Take this with you—just in case."

Surprisingly, before taking the knife, she hugged him. "Thank you, Edmond. No matter what happens, I will never forget this." Then she stepped back, her gaze lingering on him. The sunlight caught her eyes; there was something soft in them, behind all the pain and worry. Her fingers gently brushed his arm, but then the moment broke. She seized the knife and ran into the woods.

Edmond watched her go, sunlight filtering through the trees, illuminating her brown hair. He felt faintly apprehensive; he was helping her save her brother, he prayed she didn't think there was any more to it. He preferred a more seasoned and capable woman. He was likely overthinking things.

Edmond sighed and went to go look around the tree he'd been hiding behind. The Jhorians were still there; it appeared they were taking turns going on short patrols around just the main farmhouse—all, that is, except their commander, who stood on the porch, watching everything. Edmond knew little about Jhorian rankings, but the man held himself differently. He had markings of symbols on the side of his breastplate, and all of the others went to him after coming back from their short patrols.

The moments stretched on, longer than they should have. He felt time drag as he watched them. Edmond shifted anxiously, trying not to move until Petra was in position, though he worried too much time had passed; then again, the Jhorians had shown no inclination to alter their current patterns either. He leaned against the tree, feeling a little calmer, but still watching everything carefully, his gaze switching between the Jhorians and the farm's landscape behind them.

Then he finally saw Petra carefully lean out from behind a storage shed near the farmhouse and wave. He smiled. She'd done well, scared and untrained as she was. But now the hard part was coming, he prayed her courage would hold, for their one hope in saving her brother depended on it. Edmond sighed, his jaw clenching, then he pushed himself away from the tree before walking toward the road that led to the farm. It was time.

. . . . . .

Leonhard struggled against the ropes holding him, trying to hear what was going on outside, as terror gripped him. The sound of fighting had started moments ago; men shouted back and forth, and steel clanged against steel. He couldn't hear Petra's voice amid the mess of sounds. He was sure his family was somehow behind this. None of them would ever leave him—even if it meant their deaths. But he didn't want them to come back for him; it was better he ended up in the hands of a Jhorian

Inquisitor than any of his family, especially his sister. He strained to listen, trying to calm himself to discern what was happening.

Earlier he couldn't hear or see anything at all, because of the band of cloth they'd covered his face with. Their commander had been nice enough to explain—in a hate-filled, chilling monotone—it would blind and deafen him so that he wouldn't be able to Weave. He'd figured out how to remove it, though it didn't actually stop him from Weaving—it just made it harder, because he couldn't see or hear. He had eventually turned his faint light trick into a small fire and burned the cloth. Leonhard's singed ear was more than a fair trade for his sight and hearing, not that he could see anything lying bound on the floor like he was. He had tried burning the bindings holding him, too, but they were stronger, and if he ever got the chance to escape, he'd need his hands, so he couldn't risk them getting burned.

The back door to their farmhouse creaked open; it was back by the kitchen and his father had never gotten around to fixing it. Strange how his mind held onto such things in hard times. Familiar footsteps came rushing toward him; they were twins and knew each other's every sound. She knelt by him, and he felt a knife tugging at the ropes binding him. "Leonhard, I'm here! We'll get you out, I promise."

"Petra! You shouldn't be here. They will catch you too. Please leave!" He wanted to cry, just thinking about what would happen if they walked in to find her.

She looked at him sternly, but her eyes were sensitive. "I am not leaving you."

Leonhard could tell she wasn't changing her mind. He knew that tone of voice all too well. "Hurry, I don't know what's going on out there, but we need to go." He looked toward the front door. "I didn't hear anyone we know. Where is everyone? Mom and Dad?"

She paused, cutting his bindings and gently touching his cheek. Her voice sounded sadder than he'd ever heard it. "They're all gone, Leonhard. It's just us now..."

Leonhard choked, feeling something inside he could only describe as heartbreak. "What?! How? The Jhorians?"

She nodded. "Hush now, you're almost free. We need to go." She sighed heavily and looked toward the door, trying to listen, then the ropes holding him snapped loose. "You're free! There will be time to grieve later. We need to go now, come on."

The door slammed open and sunlight flooded into the dim interior, highlighting the armored form of the Jhorian commander. The sword he was holding dripped blood on the floor as he rushed forward. "You! Both of you godless witches die today!" He was on them fast, and though Petra tried to turn toward him with the knife she was holding, he grabbed her first and pulled her up by her hair, bringing his bloody sword toward her.

She screamed, struggling and terrified, still holding the knife and trying to turn in the man's grip. "No!"

Leonhard reacted without thinking, throwing the small fiery trick he now knew how to Weave at the man's eyes. "Let go of her, Jhorian bastard!"

The man screamed, dropping both Petra and his sword. "Godless witch!" He started spinning in circles and flailing, trying to find them. "I'll kill both of you! Sinners!"

Leonhard closed his eyes, too afraid to look, and screamed wordlessly, hurling every flame he could Weave in the man's general direction. The Jhorian continued to scream as things crashed and broke around them.

Petra pulled at his arm. "Leonhard! Come on, we have to go now! Run!"

Chapter Eighteen:
Aftermath

"Mewn rhyfel, mae buddugoliaeth a threchu yn achosi poen.
In war, both victory and defeat cause pain."
-Old Cathyoran Saying

Petra wrapped her arms around Edmond and hugged him hard, burying her face in his chest and weeping uncontrollably, her breath hitching and her chest shuddering. She didn't care that Leonhard could see her, or what he thought about it. There was too much pain over the loss of their family and joy over her brother being alive warring inside of her. She didn't know what else to do, so she cried.

Edmond grunted in pain as she hugged him. He had taken on more cuts and bruises in their final confrontation with the Jhorians. In truth, all three of them had, though not all their wounds were things you could see. He wrapped his arms around her and silently held her. Once Petra thought she could control herself enough to speak, she looked up at him. "Thank you for everything. I'll always remember what you did for us."

Finally, she stepped back and their eyes met. Edmond nodded and put his hands on her shoulders. "You're both welcome. I couldn't leave you in that situation."

Leonhard looked over at them from his spot on the road. "Thank you. I don't think we could have survived without your help." He went awkwardly quiet, unsure what else to say.

Edmond nodded to him, then looked back at Petra. "Remember what I told you. Leave now to avoid the Inquisitor, stay off the main road, and find the Drunken Bear in Talberston's Crossing. Irmina will help you find a ship. When you two reach Sceotan, look for Rosalie."

Petra nodded, meeting his eyes and smiling. "I won't forget, I promise, thank you."

"Take care of each other and be careful." Edmond smiled and squeezed her shoulders. "I want to hear stories in a few years about the Geisterschwert twins!"

Petra hugged him again. "Do you have to go? Can you not come with us?" She knew he couldn't. They talked about their plans after the battle yesterday. The conversation helped distract them from the act of burying the rest of her family. Edmond had his own path, the Aedonian army, where he planned to show other men right from wrong and eventually become a knight. Petra hoped he succeeded. Edmond was one of the only solid things she had left on Innatraea. He was a good man with a strong heart, and he could do it. She just hated seeing him go. She needed him. He gently put a hand on the back of her head and kissed her forehead.

Leonhard spoke, placing a hand on her shoulder. "Come on, Petra, Edmond has his own path and so do we. It's time to go. We need to get moving before more Jhorians arrive."

Edmond stepped back and Leonhard pulled her away at the same time. She wiped her eyes and tried to put on a brave smile. "I know, we will all be alright now!"

Edmond smiled and tucked a stray strand of hair behind her ear. "Take care of yourself, Petra Geisterschwert."

Petra had the urge to follow him as he walked away, but Leonhard's hand on her shoulder held her steady. When Edmond reached the last bend in the road, Petra broke free from her brother's grip and took a few steps forward. "Edmond!" He stopped and turned to look back at her. "I want to hear stories too! About Ser Carlon!"

He smiled and waved. "You will!" And then he was gone.

Petra swayed on her feet, unmoored, but Leonhard was there again, steadying her with a hand on her shoulder. She looked down the road that once led to their farm, then north, the direction where Edmond had gone, and finally turned to look at her brother. It was time to go; there was nothing here for them anymore. Their whole family was gone, the farmhouse had burned, and Petra couldn't work a farm by herself, let alone build a new home.

What was she going to do, marry? After what they had been through, she believed most men's hearts were murky and shadowed at best. Petra couldn't see herself trusting a man, let alone loving one. She looked north again, thinking, *well, not just any man.*

"Be strong, child of Cathyor. You have risen. The roots of destiny have your heart now." Petra wiped her tears away and nodded. Things had been impossibly hard, and they'd struggled through insurmountable pain, but there was a new life ahead for all of them.

She turned back to Leonhard and smiled. Her brother becoming a Weaver was what mattered now. It was time to go. She started walking. "Come on, Leonhard, let's get you to Sceotan."

. . . . . .

Caleb's breath rasped as he stumbled out of the now burned shell that used to be a farmhouse. He fell to his knees under the morning sun, partly due to weakness and partly because of what he saw there. The godless witch boy had taken his left eye, along with what felt like the rest of his face, but the limited field of vision he still had was more than enough. His men, the anointed of Jhoras, lay rotting in the farmyard. They'd been cut to pieces by a sinner wielding a magic blade and left for the crows, which now cloaked their bodies in a frenzy of black, fluttering wings. Eleven anointed of Jhoras, almost an entire Fist, destroyed by sinners. It was beyond shameful.

Caleb turned his gaze to the storage shed they had put Ethan's body in. You did not bury the anointed in godless lands but instead took them back to Porto de la Luce for a ceremonial burial. The door was broken open, and he could hear coyotes barking inside. Everything in this godless land seemed to be against them.

He would find the sinners. That godless witch boy, his wretched sister, and that young swordsman, too. He would find them and bathe in their blood before the end. He would add their blood, proof of their deaths, to the cloth he carried, in the name of Jhoras. There was no mercy for murderers, sinners like these deserved the worst fate imaginable. Caleb reached down to his belt, seeking out the red-stained cloth, resisting the pain. It felt like his skin was made of fire, like his clothing had been burned into his very being. His fingers touched nothing but ash.

Caleb wanted to scream, but he was an anointed of Jhoras and a commander, so instead he lowered his head and closed his eyes to quietly pay respect to the dead and pray to Jhoras for guidance. "Fratros, Joranem manum vos sanum trovus, et Joranem voluntatem ego in vita trovem." Brothers, may you find peace in Jhoras's hand, and I find his will in this life.

Caleb forced himself to his feet. Weakness coursed through him, but his will was stronger than what the godless had done to him and his men. He stumbled over to the nearest corpse, his brother, flailing around savagely and yelling to scare the crows away from their scavenging. It was Edriel. The man's lack of imagination and intellect had always bothered Caleb, but he was an anointed and they were brothers. Caleb fell to his knees by the man and gently closed Edriel's eyes with his hand, trying to ignore that one of his eyes was now a vacant hole.

Caleb took the man's Sica, Jhoras's divine dual-edged dagger. As the sole survivor of their war against these sinners, it was his job to take the men's Sica and use the blades to inflict Jhoras's Will upon their enemies. He also took the man's belt and ripped a piece of the man's shirt away, tucking it into the belt after wrapping it around his waist. Caleb pushed himself up and stumbled toward the next corpse. He wouldn't bury them. Jhoras had already borne witness to their failures, and judgement came for all men. He would take their Sica and follow those sinners to the ends of Innatraea, if necessary, and make them pay for his men's shame and their lives.

Sometime later Caleb stopped on his way out of the farmyard to stare at his reflection in a blood-reddened puddle of water. He looked like a wretched sinner, despite taking some of the other men's clothing. They didn't hide his charred flesh or mangled features, now haunted by loss. So be it. Though mortal Innatraeans may judge him for his appearance, Jhoras knew his true worth. His hand drifted over the hilts of the six Sica—his own and one for each slain anointed brother he had found— now hanging at his belt. He wished Gideon's Sica was among them. The man had been his brother for a long time; they had even become anointed together. Caleb would see Jhoras's divine will done.

CHAPTER NINETEEN: GWYDIR WOOD

Edmond closed his eyes, enjoying the warm crackling campfire and thinking over his journey so far. Finding out about his parents, leaving home, and separating from his friends had been so hard. But meeting Irmina and Petra, despite the extreme challenges that had led to both, had been wonderfully surprising events. One of those women had taught him the value of intimacy and sharing one's heart, while the other had shown him how strong he could be. He had learned a lot from both and would never forget either woman.

Then there was what he'd done for Petra, killing those men, the Jhorians. A part of him felt he should be more troubled by the lives he'd taken—but they had tried to do worse to Petra, and had slaughtered most of her family simply because they believed Weaving was wrong. Edmond knew better, because he had grown up around Rosalie and Crilla. Killing those Jhorians felt more like justice than anything shameful, especially considering what his grandmother had told him about his family.

But what really haunted Edmond's thoughts was the voice he'd been hearing, the voice he knew to be his mother's. Then there was his father's sword and the power it had. What did it all mean? Who was he really? There was no way he was just the random son of a small noble house. That didn't make sense, no matter how he looked at it. Though one thing he was sure of was that life had been simpler back home, before he'd had any inkling of the truth.

These thoughts had really come to a head yesterday when he'd been standing at the last bridge over the Victory River while on his was to Bethseda. There was an old, unmaintained road that led northeast to where he didn't know, so Edmond started walking toward Bethseda instead. His mother's voice had come into his mind again. "Cian, my son. Go the other way. The truth is waiting for you. Look for Gwydir Wood." He paused in shock, staring down at his dusty-booted foot, as if where it landed held the answers.

Edmond changed course immediately and before too long he found an old beaten-up sign post with "Gwydir Wood" written on it. He had made camp, caught a few ground birds, and roasted them. He was exhausted and was getting ready to lay down for the night, but he wanted answers. He looked out into the dark forest around him. Was his mother still alive? Was she here? The night was eerily quiet in response and exhaustion finally won over his desire to stay awake for the truth.

The night was darker than it should be, and their small cabin was burning, engulfed in flames that echoed Edmond's confusion. His grandmother, now a gaunt and sad-looking ethereal giant, looked down at him from the darkness. Her tears changed into blood as she spoke. "Edmond, I am not your grandmother."

Some part of himself knew this was a dream, a memory, but he was unable to wake himself. The sky grew darker, and it started to rain. He knew that the rain, too, was his grandmother's tears. "Your parents, they were a very small Cathyoran house, royalty, but not influential. I was their biume, and so it was my duty to protect you." The giant apparition of his grandmother opened her eyes: They looked like mournful voids. "When the Jhorians attacked, your parents bade me flee, to take you and the sword to safety. I kept this a secret until now to protect you. Forgive me, Edmond, please?" She caught on fire then, burning along with what used to be their home.

Edmond screamed into those flames, tears of desperation streaming down his cheeks. "Who... am... I... ?! Who am I?!"

Edmond woke with a start, gasping, chest tight, body trembling. "Cian, be calm now, my son. I am here."

After he had calmed down, Edmond looked out into the night, but there was still no one there. He shivered and looked at the campfire he'd set earlier, but it was mere embers and held no warmth. He was not going to fall back asleep, so he got up to gather wood to rekindle the fire. A sound came to his ears. It was the sound of stormy wind and creaking tree branches, and the sound echoed all around him.

Edmond stopped and picked up his sword, his hand resting on the hilt as he looked out into the dark night. The gap between life and death was a very small thing, sometimes all you had was your ability to stay alert and react quickly. He wasn't expecting a threat, his mother's voice had led him here, after all, and he couldn't believe she meant to harm him. At the same time, he had no idea what to actually expect. He'd never been one for the spiritual or magical side of things. Edmond had always preferred the blade and his wits. He found himself wishing that Jonaas or Rosalie were here; they would know what to do.

The sound of creaking tree branches and wind swelled, picking up tempo and coming closer to him. Edmond squinted, peering into the night, but the darkness hid everything. The forest stilled as a strange silence descended around him. From too loud to utter stillness, Edmond felt the hairs on his neck stir and he pulled his sword out just enough to bare some of the blade and make drawing it faster. He spun in circles, looking for anything and everything at the same time, but the still darkness revealed nothing to either his eyes or ears.

But then he saw it. Two huge glowing eyes above the tree line, staring straight at him, lighting the darkness like magic. In shock he stepped back, dropping his sword and tripping over his knapsack. The eyes moved as he did, faster than he could ever run. What came out of the trees shocked him even more.

She was much taller than the trees, beautiful, terrifying, and coming right for him. The forest creaked and moved with her as if she was a part of it. A word echoed in the back of his mind, an ancient story he'd heard Jonaas and Rosalie talking about once: Dryads.

She knelt in front of Edmond and her giant magically glowing eyes met his gaze as her face lowered toward his. The greenish purple depths of her giant eyes regarded him with calm curiosity. Edmond trembled in fear, his knees buckling.

She spoke with a startlingly lilting voice that echoed with the wind and forest's creaking movement like music, blowing over him like a strong breeze. "Your blood sings to me, son of Cathyor. Who are you?" A strange insistence lingered on the word "son," as if it held deeper meaning.

Edmond shivered in fear and swallowed nervously. "Edmond..."

"Is that who you think you are? Edmond Carlon from Aliselle Falls? You are more."

Edmond almost forgot his fear, mind reeling. What? How did a Dryad know anything about him? Who was he? "I don't know." His mind scrambled for another answer, barely remembering what his grandmother had revealed and what his mother had called him, and sighed. If this was what would lead him to the truth, then so be it. Edmond met the Dryad's piercing gaze, trying to stay calm and look brave. "Cian. What that name means, I do not know."

Twinkles of glowing amber appeared in those eyes, followed by soft, lilting laughter, and then she smiled. Everything surrounding Edmond calmed with her amused smile, and he felt a strange peace settle upon himself. If she wanted to hurt him, they wouldn't be talking, and he was sure she knew who he was. "You have done well, child of Cathyor. The wind and trees, the roots of destiny, they all listen to you."

She paused, as her eyes weighed his very soul, and she tilted her head to the side, listening to something he couldn't hear. She looked back at him and nodded, as if she had confirmed something. "There is someone here who wishes to speak with you. A woman who died long ago, but her soul still touches Innatraea. She has been waiting for you, Edmond, son of Cathyor. Your mother. If you trust me, I can take you to her."

Again he noticed that strange insistence on the word "son," but she seemed earnest, as much as a giant Dryad could, at least. If she wanted to hurt him, she could have already easily destroyed him without a second thought. Edmond got to his feet and nodded, trying to remain calm. "Yes, please take me to her!" His voice sounded too loud and rushed to his ears, so he paused and took a deep breath, trying to calm himself. "Thank you."

Roots came out of the ground and grasped hold of him, Edmond breathed deeply, trying to calm his quickly beating heart. Other roots formed a hollow circle in front of him, and then the Dryad's giant hand gently touched the top of his head. Edmond felt something of himself pass through that circle, even though his body didn't actually move. Innatraea changed around him; it was similar but everything had a subtle glow around it, like magic.

What really drew his attention, though, was the woman standing a short ways from him. She was beautiful and tall, with long wavy brown hair and hazel eyes. Her posture radiated someone who knew her own power and expected the obedience of Innatraea herself. She smiled and came to him, wrapping her arms around Edmond and hugging him against herself. One of her hands stroked his hair gently as she kissed the top of his head, crying. "Cian, my son..."

Edmond stood there, unsure what to say or do. "Mother...?"

She stepped back as her hands traced every visible cut and bruise on his face and arms before coming to rest upon his shoulders. "Your voice brings joy to my heart, but we only have a short time. Rhosynd is powerful, but even her magic has its limits." She smiled, pure love and joy showing in her eyes, as she squeezed his shoulders and straightened his shirt. "You have become a man, Cian. I am so proud of you."

"Mother... Who am I?"

She put a hand on his cheek, gently touching the wound he had there now. Her eyes became more serious. "You are Cian Ahearne, son of Isolde and Cormac Ahearne, prince heir of Cathyor."

The words hit Edmond like lightning. Though he'd had his suspicions he was someone important, this confirmation shocked him to his core. He felt himself sway, but Isolde, his mother, wrapped her arms around him again.

"I am... a prince?"

"You are whatever you choose to be, my son." She kissed his forehead. "Our Cathyor was a beautiful place, and losing her wounded us all, but you are alive and that is enough for my heart." She stepped back again, her hands on his shoulders, and met his eyes. "Rwy'n dy garu di." I love you.

He smiled, trying to be brave and return this woman's feelings, his mother's feelings, not knowing how else to honor her. "I love you too... mother."

Her fingers traced the small birthmark on his shoulder, by his neck, the one that had always reminded him of a horse head. "You have been marked as an Ahearne. That is good." She hugged him again, crying. "Our time draws short, my son. Know that I, and all of Cathyor, are always with you." She stepped back, becoming more ethereal. "With the last of me I mark you myself, as Trefn Cyfiawnder, my son. Rwy'n dy garu di."

Her body faded, turning into small glimmers of glowing magical light in front of Edmond's eyes. He held out his hand, feeling tears running down his cheeks. "Mother...?" The glimmers floated toward him, settling on his hand as they started burning. Edmond pulled his hand back as it trembled, and he gasped in pain. When he looked down at it there was a new mark there, burned into his flesh, a tree and sword.

Then something pulled him back into himself, and Edmond was again looking into the Dryad's giant eyes. She smiled. "A last gift for you, son of Cathyor. A Glamor, to hide you from your enemies until you are ready."

Light bathed Edmond and he closed his eyes. Then, moments later, the forest returned to normal. An owl hooted in the distance, and he opened his eyes. He looked down at his right hand, where the glimmers of his mother's magic had burned him. The mark wasn't there, but as he touched his hand, he felt the sting of pain from it being burned into his flesh. It reminded him of the symbol he had seen on Petra's cloak.

Edmond looked into the night. His mother's words echoed through his thoughts. Cathyor. Was that what had been calling him? Pulling him to a road he didn't know? What was he supposed to do now? Bring back his parents' people? Were they not his people too? Or maybe his duty was to destroy not just the Jhorians but also their Aedonian allies, for what they'd done to his people's kingdom. How could he enlist now, knowing this?

Edmond stood there thinking, staring into the night. "Let your feet follow your heart, until you find your place of resurrection." Where did his heart belong now? How could he follow it when he had no idea who he really was? What was he supposed to do? The night dragged on as Edmond searched within himself for the answers, but they didn't come.

Chapter Twenty: The Cruelty of Faith

"Mae ein calonnau yn tyfu fel gwreiddiau, ac yn gwaedu fel drain.
Our hearts grow like roots, and bleed like thorns."
-Old Cathyoran Saying

Leonhard stared into the darkening evening, thinking. He watched the nearby ravine's shadows lengthen. A deep feeling of guilt and sadness had formed within him, and he didn't know what to do with that. Their whole family had been killed, simply because he had been born able to Weave. More than that, though, it was actually because he'd not understood how truly dangerous his abilities were and had been showing his sister. Their family died not because he could Weave, but because the Jhorians saw him. How was he supposed to live with that?

He looked at Petra, his twin sister. She was turning the rabbits they'd caught over on their fire. He still could not believe she found help and had come back for him. What did she see when she looked at him? Her brother? Or the monster who'd gotten their whole family killed? She had always been much stronger than him, and these horrible events had proven that. He still found it unbelievable what she had been able to do on her own. His sister was a warrior.

Petra looked up and met his eyes, her gaze becoming stern and worried, a combination she had long since mastered, especially where it concerned him. She picked up a small rock and threw it at him. "Stop it, right now."

Leonhard leaned forward, resting his chin on his hands, gazing into the fire. "I didn't do anything."

He could almost hear her exasperation and rolling eyes. "You're blaming yourself for what happened. None of this was your fault, Leonhard."

"He looked up, his throat tight, tears falling. "How can you say that? If they hadn't seen me everyone would still be alive! Mom and Dad..."

Petra's voice rose, sharp with anger. "Stop being an idiot. What were you supposed to do? Pretend you are a normal Innatraean your whole life?!"

"But if they hadn't seen me..."

"Someone would have eventually. I should have taken you to Sceotan as soon as we knew." She looked down and closed her eyes; her shoulders shook, and she started crying quietly. "Maybe it's my fault."

Leonhard looked at her, shocked. "No! You can't blame yourself for what I am!"

Petra opened her eyes and wiped her nose. "It was the Jhorians and their mercy. I'll never understand how a faith can value cruelty like the Jhorians do. Everything is their fault!" She gazed into Leonhard's eyes, a very serious look coming over her. "Promise me we won't blame ourselves. It was them, and we'll make them pay for it some day!" She reached her hand out.

Leonhard took it, and they both nodded. "I promise. Someday they'll answer for it."

Petra handed him one of the skewered rabbits. "Eat. We both need to keep our strength up. We still have a long way to travel. Sceotan is very far away."

He took a bite of the rabbit, then looked at her and smiled. It was time to change the subject. They both needed at least a little happiness; even if he didn't deserve it, his sister did. "You should put me on a ship and then head north."

Petra arched an eyebrow at him. "Why would I do that? We've always stuck together."

Leonhard wiggled his eyebrows in the way that used to always make her laugh. "Edmond went that way!"

Petra's eyes widened and she lowered the rabbit she'd been about to bite into. "He's just a friend, nothing more!"

Leonhard calmly took another bite of rabbit and chewed while watching his sister's face do some very interesting things. "I'm sure he'd be more than happy to see you again."

She finally looked down and spoke, trying to sound calm, though her hands betrayed her—nervously twisting the stick that held her rabbit. "He's just a friend, Leonhard, and probably one we will never see again."

"I think we will see him again."

Petra looked up, meeting his gaze. "What makes you say that?"

"No one shows up and does what he did for us to just disappear. I'm sure we're connected somehow."

Petra smiled, her voice almost a whisper. "I hope so."

"I knew it!"

She threw another small rock at him. "Eat your rabbit! We have a long day ahead of us tomorrow. You need rest and so do I. We should have no problem reaching Talberston's Crossing, but then we'll need to find Irmina and a ship."

Leonhard only nodded, his hunger finally winning over his sadness and urge to cheer Petra up. Sceotan. Everything that mattered to his sister now was about him reaching Sceotan, because he was going to be a Weaver and they were all each other had. But he was not sure. They knew little of Innatraea beyond their farm—a life that had been taken from them—and though he wouldn't admit it to her, the Weavers frightened him. How was he supposed to become one of them and battle the guilt he felt all alone? Leonhard was worried he would always need Petra. He looked across the fire at her eating; she was so much stronger than he'd ever been and ever would be. He would find a way to give her a life that made her happy. She deserved that, even if he didn't.

. . . . . .

Martin reined in his horse. He seldom thought of himself as Martin anymore—not since he had become Inquisitor Durand. When a man became anointed, he kept his name, but becoming an Inquisitor meant his very soul belonged to the Will of Jhoras. It was a great honor that required certain understandings of the work required, and a new name. These last few days, however, almost made him wish he was still simply Martin.

He sighed and took the holy pendant that hung around his neck out of his robes to examine it. It had pulsed, a feeling he was attuned to and knew it meant a Weaver had been detected. He didn't even glance at the line of other anointed halting behind him; the men knew their place and would do as required, service to Jhoras required no recognition. Instead, he stared into the pendant's amber-blue glow, carefully observing its inner lines and lights to interpret their message.

While he tried to focus on the pendant his mind went to the carriage he knew would be slowing down at the end of their line. There were three dead anointed inside, slain by the godless witch of a Trefn Cyfiawnder he had failed to capture in Haversfjord. It was shameful and embarrassing. He was used to much better results, and the situation was infuriating. He wanted to slay them all; they were dogs and sinners, nothing more.

But thus far his only recompense was the knowledge of Trefn Cyfiawnder's survival. Now, however, maybe that would change. Was this the young red-headed Weaver he'd been chasing before, or the one the other anointed had detained at the farm up ahead? The pendant indicated the Weaver was somewhere off the road west of them. There was only one way to find out. He looked back at the line of anointed behind him. "Cassian!"

Cassian was their venator; it was his job to scout, track, and hunt as needed. The man was crass and leaned toward sin more than Durand appreciated, but he knew his work and always did what was required.

Cassian sauntered up, his swagger grating, passing the rest of their line on his mangy horse and stopped nearby. Durand had to consciously force himself to not cover his nose—the horse was almost as much an insult to decency as the man himself. "You called, Inquisitor?"

Durand pointed at the trees toward the hill they had been riding past. "There is a Weaver that way, and not very far. Go find out what we're dealing with."

Cassian nodded, his lumpy face forming a cruel smile. He did love their work, if only it were in the manner of an anointed and not a sinner. "Yes, Inquisitor, right away."

Durand watched the uncouth man tie his horse to a nearby tree before sneaking off into the woods. Horses made too much noise for scouting and weren't agile enough on heavily forested ground. In truth, Cassian was very good at his work, and Durand knew that it attracted a certain sort of Innatraean, so he suffered the man's minor sins. He also heard Tytus, commander of the anointed with them, ordering his men to dismount and ready themselves. Apprehending a Weaver had some very specific requirements, such as not using armor or horses. Armor was too hard to get off if you caught fire and horses could panic at the sight of magic. Not all anointed were as strict as they were, but there was a reason they were the ones with him on most of his missions.

Waiting for Cassian to return would take time, and it was always an annoyance to him, even though he understood and respected the man's penchant for caution. The feeling was especially poignant now, because of his failure in Haversfjord and the slain anointed. Someone needed to pay for those crimes; the Will of Jhoras demanded it. Durand sighed, his jaw clenching, and dismounted, handing his reins to Tytus, who simply passed them onto another man whose name Durand didn't know. "Are the men ready?"

Tytus nodded respectfully. The man was far too studious and boring but had a very good grasp of tactics and command. "Yes, Inquisitor."

As they waited for Cassian to return, Durand's mind retraced recent events, weighing them. He wanted to kill that godless Trefn Cyfiawnder witch, but at least he had stabbed her, and more than once. She had a long road to recovery ahead of her, and the idea of the witch suffering for her sins against Jhoras made Durand smile to himself, until he remembered the slain anointed. The godless witch needed to burn for her sins!

Of even graver concern, however, was the Weaver they'd failed to capture. The descriptions he'd been able to glean, from the other inn patrons, said she was very young but handled herself well, had curly red hair and green eyes. He assumed she must be a Legacy, which meant there could be more Weavers within the region. There was no sin against Jhoras more severe than Weaving. Innatraeans were not meant to wield that kind of power. He would find this godless witch too, and take her to Porto de la Luce where she belonged, in chains.

Lastly there was the Geisterschwert family. He'd received word days ago that the anointed sent to assist him in Haversfjord had found and detained a Weaver on this family's farm. Was that who his pendant had detected? Or was it both of them? Capturing two Weavers would be fortuitous indeed. The situation, though, still did not bode well. Durand started rubbing his chin, deep in thought. Multiple Weavers, a possible Legacy, the Trefn Cyfiawnder witch, and the loss of his fellow anointed. The rot in this region festered, and he needed to know why.

Cassian finally appeared at the tree line and gave him a series of hand signals. There were only two sinners, a boy and a girl, and the boy was the godless witch of a Weaver his pendant had detected. He looked at Tytus, who had also seen the signals and knew their meaning. "Move in, seize the boy first, slay the girl. I'm going with you."

CHAPTER TWENTY-ONE: RHOSYND

"Dryad a Choeden, llafn a chalon,
mae'r rhain yn gwneud Trefn Cyfiawnder beth yw hi.
Dryad and Tree, blade and heart,
these make a Trefn Cyfiawnder what she is."
-Scatha Cadain

This time Petra's nightmare was similar yet even more terrifying. The sun burned black, mirroring the rot in men's souls. One of the Jhorians dragged her cousin Claudia away and behind the nearby barn, his pure white tabard and shining steel armor reflecting the blackness, with the three-quartered cross on his chest bleeding. It was not long after that Claudia started to scream. Petra looked up from her place on the ground, where she was bound in steel chains next to her brother, and shuddered. There was blood everywhere. She laid her head down, not wanting to see more, then someone shoved her face into the mud. Petra struggled to look beside her, to see her brother, but he wasn't there; it was only a shadow...

She knew it was a dream, but Petra could not wake, it was as if the nightmare had her very soul. Her body shook with the memories of terror and sadness, but the visions wouldn't let her go.

"Wake, child of Cathyor! They are coming!" Her body shook. Petra could hear the voice inside of her dreams. She knew it meant danger, but the terror wouldn't let her go.

Edmond tucked a stray strand of hair behind her ear and smiled. "Take care of yourself, Petra Geisterschwert."

A droplet of water fell from the sky, dissolving Edmond as if he were only a reflection, a ghost of her past desires. She held out her hand. "No! Don't go! Stay with me. Please?"

Then the water rippled as vines and roots coursed through it, somehow forming a sword.

"Wake!"

This time the voice boomed through Petra's being, shaking her like thunder, and her eyes shot open. She tried to move, but there was something holding her down. Vines? No, ropes. Petra raised her head enough to look around. Her heart trembled and her chest tightened at what she saw. Jhorians surrounded their camp, and they already had Leonhard tied like before—even Petra was bound. How did they manage to find them? They had been careful to choose a spot not visible from the road. How had they snuck up and bound them both without making noise? Terror gripped Petra as she frantically looked around for a way out.

A cruel voice laughed from near her. "You're caught, godless witch, and your brother is ours." A hand touched her head. "Don't worry, I'll make sure you are nice and taken care of before the end."

Petra reeled inside, despair and hopelessness taking hold of her. "Call the roots, child of Cathyor. Do not fear, embrace your power."

Petra took a deep breath. They only had each other, she and Leonhard, which meant that she had to do this. Petra felt something beyond her fear, something she remembered from a place deep inside, like a secret brought into the sunlight. The ground beneath her moved, as roots came out and grasped the ropes holding her, snapping them apart. As Petra shot to her feet, she snatched the knife from the belt of the man who'd spoken and slit his throat in the same motion, barely noticing that he was dressed more like a woodsman than a Jhorian.

A wind blew through the camp as other Jhorians yelled their obscenities and came for her. The wind blew Petra's cloak around her, and she pulled the hood up, disappearing from their sight. She rushed through the camp to get to Leonhard, avoiding the confused Jhorians. One of them stepped into her path and she slipped to the side, taking his knife in her other hand as she did. In that moment of pure fury and desperation, Petra remembered something her uncle had taught her about butchering. The Jhorian's knife slid into the man's side, piercing his heart and dropping him instantly as she dashed for her brother.

Suddenly a fist hit Petra in the gut hard, knocking the wind out of her. As she stumbled a man stepped in and backhanded her even harder, snapping her head to the side and making her drop the knives she had taken. His hand closed around her neck as he lifted her off the ground and ripped her cloak away. "Trefn Cyfiawnder witch! Not all servants of Jhoras are so easily tricked. You are mine!"

Petra flailed and fought, putting all she had into trying to free herself. But he was too strong for her and bigger than she was. "Leonhard!"

The man started walking, carrying her as if she weighed nothing, smiling cruelly. "I am Inquisitor Durand, and I will be taking your godless witch brother with me to Porto de la Luce." He shook her violently. "You however, Trefn Cyfiawnder witch, I will start cleansing the rot of this land with your death." He stepped to the edge of the ravine near their camp. "I hope you survive the fall, godless witch. Then you can imagine your brother's fate in the hands of Jhoras while you bleed to death." And with that, he dropped her.

Everything slowed as she fell. Petra could feel hope and life fading with each heartbeat. In pure utter desperation she reached for the Inquisitor, trying to hold onto life, but she was too late—or too far away. Petra plummeted downward, hitting bushes, branches, and rocks on her way down. She knew this meant not only her certain death, but also Leonhard's; they were both done. Petra rolled into a ball, vainly hoping she'd somehow survive and not break every bone in her body. The ravine's deep shadows swallowed her whole as hope itself receded above. Petra closed her eyes and waited for the end.

After a brutal strike against a rock, the air around her changed. Sound seemed to fade away, and a strange peace fell over her. "I have you, child of Cathyor." Petra felt two giant hands cradle her body, slowing the fall, as a pressure like the heavy stillness before a thunderstorm built around her. Petra felt a dizzying shift, and then she was somewhere else, laying on soft ground.

Petra leapt to her feet quickly, looking around wildly. "Leonhard?!" She didn't see her brother, and she wasn't where she was supposed to be. Everything in the forest around her glowed with its own soft light. Where was she? Where was her brother? What had happened?

"Be calm, child of Cathyor. You are safe. This world flows differently. We have time."

Petra froze. The voice was no longer inside her head. The lilting musical voice came from above her. She looked up slowly, into the beautiful purple and green eyes of a giant, who seemed to be half tree and half beautiful goddess. Petra's legs buckled. She fell to her knees in shock, heart beating fast, breath catching in her throat, mouth working silently.

"You are safe, child of Cathyor."

Petra gulped and shook herself. The voice had never guided her wrong and this might be her last chance to save Leonhard and herself. "Where am I? What are you?" Her voice trembled with weakness, but she managed to ask her questions in a rush.

The giant, who Petra noticed was sitting near her, laughed softly and with amusement. It was a musical lilting sound and spots of glowing amber flickered in her eyes. "I have been waiting for you, Petra Geisterschwert, child of Cathyor. Since the beginning of my time. I am Rhosynd, Dryad of Gwydir Wood." The Dryad smiled and didn't move otherwise. "Do not be afraid, Petra. We still have time to save your brother. This world has a different flow." She tilted her head to the side as if listening to something Petra couldn't hear. "You must listen to me and decide, with your whole heart."

Petra just sat there, too shocked and tired and beaten to know what else to do. "Where are we? What is a Dryad? Why did you help me? Can we save my brother?! He's all that I have left!"

"We are in the world that borders Innatraea, Byd Nesaf." Rhosynd smiled again and Petra realized her hair was made of leaves, roots, and vines. "We Dryads connect these worlds and are a part of them. We also keep them in balance." Rhosynd motioned with her giant hands, which Petra realized were traced with plants and glowed like everything else here as she spoke. "We can save your brother, but first you must accept your destiny, Petra, child of Cathyor."

"My destiny?" What did she have to do? She had to save Leonhard, no matter the cost.

"You are Trefn Cyfiawnder, child of Cathyor. One of many blood lines, powerful women knights whose Cyfeillach Gysegredig, or 'Sacred Bond' to the Dryads, makes them a part of Coedwig Amser, giving them the power to keep order on Innatraea."

Petra's mind recalled that phrase. The Inquisitor had called her that, and he hated her for it. What did it mean? "Dryads? Sacred Bond? Coedwig Amser?"

"Coedwig Amser, the Forest of Time, connects us all. Through every eon, the blood of your ancestors flows and connects like roots. This great forest beats with millions of hearts. Their destinies have become the legacy you each carry. Though their leaves have fallen, their knowledge still nourishes you, making you strong. The roots of Coedwig Amser are what created Trefn Cyfiawnder, Cyfeillach Gysegredig, and our power. Dryad and Tree, Heart and Blade. We are all a part of everything."

Petra didn't fully understand, but if this meant she was the enemy of men like the Jhorians and could save her brother, then so be it. Petra stood up slowly, fighting the pain and exhaustion she felt. "I'll do it."

Vines gathered on the ground before her and started intertwining into the shape of a sword as they lifted into the air. "The trees have withered, and many branches have died, but their heart and that of Cathyor still remain. This sword's name is Cangen Marw, which means

'Dead Branch,' and it is yours. She represents our bond. Take her, and together we will feed the roots with the blood of our enemies."

Petra hesitated, looking around as she tried to think. She wanted to save her brother, but was this truly a part of her destiny? More emotions surged through her than she could name. Then her eyes fell upon something in the distance, a tall, beautiful woman who looked like a queen embracing a man she recognized. Petra stepped forward without thinking. "Edmond?"

A giant hand came down in front of her, blocking her view. "You will meet him again, Petra, but not now. Your paths must diverge before they come together again."

She looked up and met Rhosynd's eyes. "What is he doing here? Will we truly meet again?"

"He is saying farewell to his mother before she leaves Byd Nesaf. Listen well, Petra, child of Cathyor. One day your paths will cross again, and his crown will rest upon your strength. Until then you must keep his name close to your heart and tell no one. This is imperative."

"His crown? Who is he really?"

Rhosynd tilted her head again, then spoke softly. "It is time, Petra. Choose with your heart. Take the blade and my bond, become who you are meant to be. Trust the roots of destiny and our connection."

Petra turned back to the strange sword made of vines, roots, and wood. She really didn't have a choice. If she had the power to save Leonhard, and if Edmond would one day depend upon her, then she had to face whoever she truly was. Petra closed her eyes and reached her hand out to grasp the hilt, unsure of what to expect but knowing it was right.

Everything changed in a mere heartbeat. Petra could feel the sword's roots and vines, but not just *in* the sword—*inside* of herself too, as if they were one. Light pierced Petra, as the vines climbed over her, permeating her body with glowing veins beneath her skin. Petra felt like a leaf as the veins of light traced her inner being and those of her ancestors through time. Her heart was a forest, beating and breathing through the very roots of her soul and those of all the women before her. Everything was connected inside of her. Petra, who she was, the sword, and Rhosynd. Within that bond was creation, within the beating of her heart and that of the forest were the roots of her past and future. Destiny. Power.

Dryad and Tree, Heart and Blade, she finally understood. Petra opened her eyes.

CHAPTER TWENTY-TWO: YR YNAD DIAL

(THE JUSTICE IN VENGEANCE)

"Mae hen hud Innatraea yn cysgu yng nghoedwigoedd mawr Cathyor, yn aros am y dydd i ddialedd a marwolaeth.
Innatraea's old magic sleeps in the great forests of Cathyor, waiting for The Day of Vengeance and Death."
-Morrigan Bresling

Elspeth lowered her head, hiding her face within her hood, as they started riding past the Jhorians. She hated them all, every last one of them deserved death at the edge of her blade. But their current situation required stealth. The Inquisitor in Haversfjord had seen her face, and that meant her description might be known, so Elspeth kept her head down. This group of Jhorians outnumbered them more than two to one, and they needed to find their prince before he was discovered by anyone else, which meant not making a scene. Though it pained her to ride past these savage men without ending them, she focused on staying calm and keeping her breathing steady. Archibald rode up beside her and silently placed his hand on her shoulder. How did the man always know?

Then she saw him coming out of the carriage the Jhorians had with them: Inquisitor Durand. Elspeth's hand went to Crogwyr's hilt immediately, and her mostly healed stab wounds seemed to pulse with renewed pain as she remembered his words during their last encounter. "I am Inquisitor Durand. Come, godless witch, you will not find me such easy prey!" The scar and his name had told her then, as it did now, that this evil man had been at the burning of Brynn. He had slaughtered so many of her sisters. Queen Isolde. Brighid. Aisling. He had to die. Heat and rage pulsed through Elspeth as she drew Crogwyr, getting ready to charge. As always, Archibald knew, but his quietly insistent voice in her ear was too late. "My love, don't!"

Elspeth leaned in, using her knees to signal Styfnig into a charge and headed straight into the Jhorian camp. She felt more than saw her companions coming after her. They were good loyal Innatraeans and would never abandon her, even when she was being reckless. It was both one of their greatest strengths and weakness, as with most things.

Elspeth struck down the first Jhorian before they even saw her coming. They'd been distracted by the carriage and settling in to cook the evening meal. The Jhorian's blood ran down Crogwyr's blade as it started to glow white with its own internal rage—the sword liked to make Jhorians bleed.

These men were better trained than those in Haversfjord had been. They were already brandishing billhooks or mauls and completely ignoring their swords, as if they knew how useless they'd be. These were men who had engaged Trefn Cyfiawnder women before and that made them dangerous. Elspeth tried to pull Styfnig to a halt and back him up, but one of the Jhorians was already within striking distance with his vicious-looking maul. She readied herself for the fall but then an arrow flew past her and struck the man in his neck, sending him to the ground. Caoimhe and Aidan were both excellent archers, and she often thanked Rhiannon for their presence, though she was never sure which one of them shot any specific opponent. Both swore she could tell, something about how the arrow feathers looked, as if she had time to check such things in open battle.

Styfnig started to back up, probably realizing the tight quarters were no place for a horse—he'd always been a smart animal. As they stepped back, Archibald and Florian ran in front of her, engaging the incoming Jhorians on foot. If the man always being there to save her wasn't so endearing, she'd be furious; he always knew and always had a plan, often rescuing Elspeth from her rash actions. If ever there was a man too stubborn and intelligent for his own good, it was Archibald Stallwood.

She dismounted and joined the fight, while Oryvn pulled Styfnig back toward the archers and their other companions pressed the attack, trying to close the gap in the lines. It was a dangerous situation, Elspeth knew, but she couldn't allow Inquisitor Durand to escape again, not this time. The man had outworn his lease on life.

Then the true fury of battle collapsed around them, surrounding them in its chaos. They were outnumbered at least three to one, and it started to show very quickly as their enemy encircled them and started pushing inward. Florian went down to a spear thrust in his gut, lowering their already slim chances of survival. Elspeth tried to clear her head of the clashing steel, blood, and yelling, surveying the field quickly. Archibald came beside her, panting. He had a new gash along his cheek and was tiring. They were getting too old for this. She looked at Archibald and nodded. He might have been right this one final time—she shouldn't have engaged them. It was too late now, but she would not travel to Byd Nesaf without taking Inquisitor Durand with her. She looked at Archibald. "Yr wyf yn dy garu, bydd i ti gael heddwch yn y Byd Nesaf." *I love you, may you find peace in the next world.*

His eyes widened, but she was already charging into the enemy lines, lifting now brightly glowing Crogwyr in front of her. "Durand!"

. . . . . .

Rhosynd screamed. It was unlike anything Petra had heard before. It was more a feeling than a sound. Her entire body vibrated with it, as loose leaves and twigs lifted into the air around her, borne by the wind of that primal scream. It blew past her and seemed to coalesce in the air, forming a murky vision of somewhere else. Through that strange portal Petra could see a battle being waged between Jhorians and a group of Innatraeans. But all of them were moving slower, like they were immersed in the murkiness of that vision. She remembered Rhosynd's words: "This world has a different flow." Petra took a deep breath, forcing herself to pause and take account of the situation. She had time, even if things did not look good.

The battle was clearly in favor of the Jhorians, who far outnumbered their opponents. Petra didn't know them, but if she could help anyone from losing to the likes of these bastards she would. But where was Leonhard? She hadn't realized she'd thought the question to Rhosynd before the Dryad answered, her voice once again coming into Petra's mind. "He is there, Petra, my child. Inside of the carriage." The vision vibrated for a moment, then became clearer. "There is more you must do here, Petra." In the short time since their bond Rhosynd had started to use her name in every conversation, like a new word she savored pronouncing; there was always that lilt of happiness in her voice when the Dryad said it. "The woman, she must survive. She, like all Trefn Cyfiawnder women, is now your sister."

Petra looked past the larger brutal engagement, which was now even more obviously in Jhorian favor as one of the other group's few combatants fell to enemy swords. There, engaged with the Inquisitor in a savage one-on-one battle, she saw the woman. She was similar in age to Petra's mother and wore a cloak with the same tree-and-sword symbol as her own. The woman's sword glowed pure white with magic.

Petra nodded. She didn't know the woman, but she understood their bond. Like her own connection to Rhosynd, this woman also had a Dryad and she needed help. Petra took a step forward, drawing Cangen Marw from the wooden sheath the sword had somehow made for itself at her waist. She could hear the vines and branches inside of the blade creaking, as though stirred by a wind. The sound echoed a dead tree limb before falling and crushing the life from someone. She could feel its hunger. Cangen Marw wanted to kill them all, to feed their blood to its roots, and she was going to help the blade do just that. Her first step turned into a walk, then a run, as Petra screamed her brother's name and barreled through the vision in front of her.

For a single heartbeat Petra seemed to encounter resistance, as if the two worlds she was stepping between didn't know what to do with her. Then her feet hit the ground in Innatraea, as the last wind from Rhosynd's scream blew past her and sound exploded everywhere, immersing her senses. Petra stumbled briefly, disoriented, as her senses and body's movement returned to normal, and then the strange other world was gone. She was in Innatraea, surrounded by the hectic fervor of battle.

That last wind that had passed her seconds ago knocked down the Jhorians around her in that moment of disorientation, giving Petra a safe landing as she righted herself. Some of the Jhorians had been using a shield formation to close with the other group's archers and were now being peppered with arrows, after their shields had been tossed aside like leaves. Petra was already running past them. It was her time now. She and Cangen Marw had to turn the tide, and quickly. "Petra, my child..." That happy sounding lilting voice echoed inside her mind. "Take them, save your family, feed the roots of destiny with our enemy's blood."

Petra could feel her sword's roots and vines emanating around her like an ethereal spider's web that obeyed her will and that of Cangen Marw's thirst for blood. Where she ran, sharp ethereal vines struck the Jhorians, slicing flesh, wrapping wrists, tripping legs, leaving them open to be cut down. The others didn't know her, but they seemed to recognize a fellow warrior and the sword's power—or maybe they just hated the Jhorians as much as Petra did. Either way, they went to work as she swept through the camp, ending the lives of the bastards she and Cangen Marw left defenseless behind her.

Then she was there, steps away from the Inquisitor's death and her vengeance... for everything. The other woman looked at Petra as she rushed into their duel, startled for a moment before recognition settled into her eyes. They didn't know one another, but they were both Trefn Cyfiawnder and could feel it in each other's presence.

Petra moved in on the Inquisitor's other side to strike him.

Her sister yelled. "Careful, he's protected!"

But Petra struck anyway, because another voice echoed inside of her mind. "His adornments, the Will of Jhoras is nothing but trinkets, remove them and end him."

"Not from me!" She felt the droplets of blood from all the previous strikes, the blood of their enemies, seep into Cangen Marw's recesses, giving sustenance to its roots. The sword broke open and the vines came and wrapped around the Inquisitor like a vice, entangling themselves through his necklace, the three-quartered cross-shaped artifact chained to his belt, and the rings on both his hands.

Then the vines broke them, pulling the jewelry off him with the glorious sound of his terrified voice. "Impossible!"

The vines and roots pulled him to his knees, crippling him as a streak of metallic glowing white flashed past. In a spray of blood, his severed head flew off as his lifeless body fell to the ground.

The vines and roots of her sword retreated into the form of her blade, and she felt Cangen Marw's essence calm, satiated by that act of justice and vengeance. Petra looked at her sister.

The other woman's eyes showed a strange mix of emotions: Triumph, relief, confusion, and behind them all, joy. "I thought that I was all alone... Who are you?"

EPILOGUE:
AILENI
(REBIRTH)

Gwendolyn Drake, the former Rhyfelfeistr, or "Warmaster," of Trefn Cyfiawnder crossed her arms and sighed heavily. She was troubled. She was getting far too old for this, training new recruits and planning a revolution. She should have been enjoying her retirement with a fine glass of Daphshire red on her estates. Instead, she was here watching a new generation of recruits train. Truthfully, though, there was no one else, and those estates had been burned along with the rest of her beloved Cathyor. So, being too old was not going to stop her from trying to make these young women the best warriors Innatraea had ever seen and then taking vengeance on both the Aedonians and Jhorians for what they had done.

She looked at the other two women standing near her, who were also watching the practice field. Both Sigridur and Lorna had come into their own since their kingdom's fall, helping Gwendolyn train the few new recruits they'd managed to find and, like her, seeking vengeance while hoping to rebuild what they had all lost. The warring emotions of those desires had become intimately familiar to them all over the years.

Gwendolyn had others to help her as well. Though these three had been mere recruits during the fall, they too had come into their own as women. Had they not been so surrounded by so much sadness, she would be proud of them—truthfully, she was anyway. Whether that made them lucky or damned, Gwendolyn wasn't sure. It was an interesting relationship, loving your sisters and wanting a bright future for them while planning to avenge the pain of all you had lost.

Hadriana, Indila, and Etheldreda were walking amongst the recruits, giving advice here or tapping a shoulder there, occasionally demonstrating how a certain move was done. Gwendolyn crossed her arms and sighed again, her eyes surveying the practice field carefully. Every woman here knew those feelings. Even the youngest amongst them had lost their family during Cathyor's final hours, or in unfortunate battles since.

What was really troubling her was something different, however, though it too was intimately connected to their loss, like everything was these days. Gwendolyn had no reason to question any of these women's honor, tenacity, dedication, or skills. The problem was how few of them there truly were. Their large practice field, where they trained every recruit, only had twenty-three women in training. Added to the six of them, that didn't even make thirty, which at one time was the size of a single basic Trefn Cyfiawnder tactical unit. There were others—those helping Morrigan, and of course Merima, who had taken to enacting her own special kind of vengeance that only Cysgod knew. How were they ever going to build enough of a force to accomplish their goals? The Aedonians and Jhorians needed to pay—and dearly—but how?

Gwendolyn almost laughed, thinking of the absurd idea Sigridur had once suggested—that they should all have babies to bolster their ranks. Training and pregnancy didn't go well together and there were few trustworthy men left on Innatraea. It didn't help that she was old enough to be a grandmother. Gwendolyn shook herself of the thought. She had lost her own daughter and husband during the fall—even thinking about creating another family made her want to weep. These were harsh times, she of all women could not give into that weakness.

Suddenly, Gwendolyn gasped as a searing heat passed over her heart, grasping her whole soul and pulling her to the southwest. Sigridur and Lorna were by her side immediately, lending their support, probably thinking she was faltering. Gwendolyn shook the younger women off her and stood tall, smiling. Sometimes, throughout the generations of Trefn Cyfiawnder, a woman of the ancient bloodlines was born with a Pwerau Cysegredig, or one of the "Sacred Powers." She was one such woman and had the gift of Synnwyr y Galon, or "Heart Sense," something she thought she would never feel again in her life. She could feel when a new sister ascended, through Cyfeillach Gysegredig, by accepting her blade and sacred bond with a Dryad.

She looked at the other two women. "One of you get horses. We ride within the hour. The other will stay here and watch over things."

Both women knew her well. The sisters of Trefn Cyfiawnder did not keep secrets from one another, and so they both answered immediately.

Lorna smiled, always the more cheerful of their group. "A new sister?!"

Sigridur, the more practical one, merely nodded. "I'll go with you. Which way?"

Gwendolyn turned, looking toward the direction where she'd felt the pull leading her. "Southwest." She snapped her fingers. "Off with you. We need to go." She closed her eyes and took a deep breath. Life wasn't easy but it eventually gave you what you needed if you persevered. "Byddaf yn dod o hyd i chi chwaer." I will find you, sister.

. . . . . .

A few days later...

Petra stared across the campfire at Leonhard and smiled. They were finally safe—for now, anyway. She turned her head to look at the six other Innatraeans gathered in the evening light with them, and to her surprise, her smile grew even wider. Petra felt a kinship with the woman named Elspeth. They were both Trefn Cyfiawnder, and that meant they were sisters, which also inferred that she could trust the others too, especially given the ferocity they'd shown in fighting the Jhorians; rage like that always had a reason.

Petra understood that hatred all too well now. They had even lost two of their own during the battle, men named Florian and Colin, for whom they had helped prepare funeral pyres and then buried the men's ashes with their weapons.

The others kept staring at her, as if she was some strange creature they did not understand. Petra understood; they were still getting to know each other, and even she was still learning about her newly accepted power.

Elspeth came to sit near them, taking Petra's hands in her own and meeting her eyes. "Petra, sister. I'm beside myself with joy to meet you." She looked away briefly, tears welling up in her eyes. "For the longest time, since Cathyor's fall, I believed that I was alone." She squeezed Petra's hands, her gaze becoming insistent. "We must talk. I have so much to tell you, and I want to know everything." She looked at Leonhard and smiled. "About you and you brother—everything."

Petra smiled, and her chest warmed. She couldn't help it. They'd been through so much hardship, but they had survived, and now she had a sister. "Of course, though I do not know much yet. No one has taught me."

Elspeth's eyes widened. "No one has taught you?" She looked toward Petra's sword. "Then how?"

Petra replied, somewhat unsure of herself as their eyes met again. "Rhosynd. She speaks to me in my mind. She chose me and guided me herself."

"Rhosynd?"

Petra looked down, speaking quietly. "My Dryad."

Elspeth gasped. "Your Dryad speaks to you, inside your mind?!"

"Don't they all do that?"

Elspeth smiled, squeezing Petra's hands. "They do not. I have never heard of such a thing. Truly remarkable."

Petra looked down with embarrassment. Elspeth was obviously an experienced warrior, while she was just a farm girl. "I don't know what to say." She squeezed Elspeth's hands back. "Thank you."

"How did you get here? The others said there was a wind and then you were just there."

"Rhosynd brought me through the other world. She opened a portal..."

Elspeth's eyes grew even wider. "She what...?!"

Then both women fell silent as a strong wind blew through the camp, followed by the loud creaking of tree branches and a pressure in the air. "I am here, Petra. My child. Come to me in the nearby woods. We will speak. Bring Elspeth with you."

Petra nodded, then looked at Elspeth, and smiled. "She's here and wants to speak with us both. Come."

Elspeth blinked and looked toward the woods nearby. "Remarkable. I am honored."

As both women got up to go, Leonhard looked over. "Petra?"

She turned back and smiled at him. "You're safe. I'll be right back, I promise." He nodded and the two women walked into the woods together.

The wind, the creaking tree branches, and the heavy pressure followed them. A short distance into the woods, Petra saw a glimmer of light ahead, like what she remembered from when this had all begun. She headed in that direction. "She's this way."

"How do you know?"

Petra looked at Elspeth questioningly and pointed with her hand. "You can't see the glimmer there?"

Elspeth looked where she pointed, concentrating. "There it is! Now that you pointed at it, I do, it's a small flash of light." She looked at Petra. "I am beginning to wonder more and more who you are."

"I'm just Petra. Come on, she's waiting for us."

Just past the glimmer, which disappeared after they neared it, the two women found themselves in a clearing in the woods. There, Rhosynd waited, smiling at them, but only the upper part of the giant Dryad's body was aboveground, as if Rhosynd was standing inside of Innatraea herself. Petra stopped and gasped. "I didn't know you could do that!"

Rhosynd smiled and nodded, then her hands came out of the ground and wrapped around Petra as they came close. The Dryad leaned down and kissed her on the forehead. "Petra, my child. You have done so well. I am proud of you."

Petra smiled and closed her eyes; she could feel the warmth of Rhosynd's hands all around her. "Thank you for everything. We wouldn't have survived without you."

"We are the same. Our hearts and roots speak to one another now." Rhosynd withdrew her hands and straightened up, and Petra opened her eyes. "Come closer, Elspeth, daughter of Cathyor. I would like to speak with you both."

Elspeth came to stand by Petra and nodded respectfully, but not before looking sideways at her with extreme curiosity and something like admiration. "I am honored and at your service, Dryad."

Rhosynd nodded happily, then her luminous eyes became more serious as small flickers of white and red floated within them. "You both hold a secret, and though you can trust one another, I must ask you to hold this secret close to your hearts." One of her hands gently touched Petra. "You know him as Edmond, and he helped save you and your brother." Her other hand touched Elspeth. "You were there for his birth and know him as Prince Cian."

Elspeth gasped and looked at Petra. "You know him?" Then she looked back at Rhosynd before laying a hand on her own heart. "He is our prince! Thank you, Rhiannon."

Petra smiled. "I do know him. He's the most honorable and heroic man I have ever met. You knew his mother? Was she your queen?"

Elspeth's eyes took on a questioning look. "She was."

"I saw her in that strange other world saying goodbye to him."

"You saw Isolde?! Fy anwyl chwaer, boed i ti gael heddwch yn y Byd Nesaf." My dear beloved sister, may you find peace in the next world.

Rhosynd silently watched the women talk, smiling. But finally, she interrupted them, resting a hand gently on each woman so they would look at her again. "Listen well. You must let the roots of destiny grow at their own pace. You cannot go to him yet, no matter how much your hearts desire it. A new path will open soon, and you must take it." Rhosynd met each woman's eyes. "Keep his secret close to your hearts. Tell no one and trust in one another."

With those last words Rhosynd faded away, and the two women were left alone in the clearing. They looked at one another, then embraced desperately, both of them crying.

· · · · ·

Weeks later...

Irmina stopped outside Agnes's small cabin, around the small path's bend, so she could take a moment to think about what she truly wanted. Agnes was their town's wise woman, though no Innatraean would ever hear a local woman say that, because the Jhorians and their Holy Church didn't abide women doing "Jhoras's work." More to the point, those soulless Jhorian bastards often called women like Agnes witches and burned them for their sins. So, the women here had learned long ago to remain silent and protect their own.

Irmina sighed. She didn't really want to be here, but sometimes even the things you hated or had given up on were a necessity. It had been years since her late husband Nathanael had passed, and they'd never been able to conceive. In truth the possibility of ever having a child had long since left her mind. There was the Drunken Bear and the girls who worked for her, but that was it. Life was simple. Even with regrets or bad memories, that was just how things were.

But then things had changed without a care about how she felt or what she wanted. A breeze washed over Irmina, causing sudden nausea. She closed her eyes and helplessly put her hands on her stomach, trying not to retch. She'd like to ring Edmond's neck and scream at him. Irmina could see the scene now: her, throttling the young man and yelling, asking him what he'd done to her. But she already knew, she could practically feel it inside of her, growing and making her feel sick. The one thing Irmina had thought she'd never have, the one thing her late husband had never given her: A baby. Did she want it?

Irmina closed her eyes, imagining how her life would be raising a child—a little one running around the inn, causing the type of havoc only children knew, breaking things, and costing her a fortune in food, clothing, and time. Surprisingly, though, she found herself smiling at those images. Children were a wonder; she and the girls were always happy when one visited their inn. Those were the happier thoughts, however. Women already had it rough in Aedonia, and raising a child by herself would be a formidable challenge. Then again, she would have the girls to help her, and if it was a boy then the inn would be inherited, keeping their family line intact.

Irmina leaned against a nearby tree and sighed. What would she ask Agnes for? Something soothing like chamomile and peppermint tea? Or a mixture of rue, myrtle, and laurel with wine? She wished Nathanael, or even Edmond, were here. The hardest part of this wasn't whether she wanted a child or not, because she did. The hardest part doing it alone, and what made this choice so very difficult. Worse still was the mix of emotions this all opened within her. When Nathanael had died, Irmina had packed all of that away, deep inside, forgetting the idea of ever loving again or having a child. Now she could have a child, but it would be alone, and, more complicated still, she was older now, so this would likely be her last chance. Tears streaked down her cheeks as these thoughts flowed through her being.

The wind picked up, blowing over Irmina and bringing the heavy feel of promise with it. For some reason this made her cry harder, so she stayed there, leaning against the tree, shedding tears of frustration and conflicting emotions. The tree above creaked in the wind, like it was swaying with her heart, to and fro, deciding what to do along with her. She smiled at the ridiculous thought—flights of fancy were not often in her nature, but it was a confusing time. Then her eyes shot open as a kind-sounding woman's voice echoed inside her mind. "Child of Cathyor, you will be a mother, and your son will change Innatraea forever."

Irmina looked around. She even stood up and looked into the brush behind the tree, then up and down the pathway. There was no one there. Who had spoken to her? Cathyor? The kingdom was gone. What did it have to do with her and the baby? A son? The voice had said she would have a son. She wasn't normally one for superstition or faith in the unseen, but what else could she call this? Had one of the Three Sisters spoken to her? Was her yet unborn child chosen by them for some purpose? A thought occurred to her: She had never really asked Edmond who he was. Was he more than just a young man traveling the road of his life? The future was uncertain, and she didn't have all the answers, but Irmina was not one to shiver in fear or take the easy path. Whatever was going to come of this, it was important and she would see it through. Irmina pushed herself up. Chamomile and peppermint tea it was.

GLOSSARY

This glossary is meant as a guide to Edmond's journey in Innatraea Novella Three: Road to Bethseda. For a more detailed series glossary, please visit www.innatraea.com

Aedonia (Ah-doh-nee-uh): A kingdom in eastern Innatraea bordering the Mu'ul Mountains known to conquer and absorb smaller nations, charge heavy taxes, enact strict laws, and is also home to the Holy Church of Jhoras.

Aerona (i-ro-na): A Dryad, bonded to Marged Llewellyn.

Agnes (ag-ness): A wise woman who provides medicine to the women of the river trade town Talberston's Crossing.

Ahearne Family (Ah-hear-neh): The ruling family of Cathyor before its fall. History claims they were all slain, though rumors persist of surviving heirs.

Ahearne family mark: A horse head-shaped mark given to the firstborn sons of House Ahearne.

Aidan (Ei-dan): A Cathyoran man, and an archer.

Aife (Ai-fe): Niomh's daughter, who is unusual because she has two different colored eyes, one blue and one green.

Ailbhe (Al-va): A Cathyoran, and a member of Trefn Cyfiawnder.

Aisling (Ash-ling): A young Cathyoran girl. Best friend of Morrigan, daughter of Brighid, and niece of Elspeth.

Aliselle Falls (Al-eh-see-ill): A farm town near the eastern border of Aedonia. It's located in the province of Farm Hold and is named after the nearby river rapids and waterfalls.

Am'ayim, "People of Sea Mist" (Am-eye-eem): The people of the Ara'ayim Isles.

Amelia: Daughter of Gisella and Herbert, sister of Sarai.

Anointed of Jhoras: Those blessed by jhoras in order to carry out his Will amongst the sinners on Innatraea.

Andrejan (on-dray-jon): A shepherd.

Archibald Stallwood (Arch-ih-bald Stall-wood): A Cathyoran man, former sergeant at arms, and current reeve of the river trade town Haversfjord.

Asherah, "Lady of the Sea" (Ash-err-ah): The mother goddess of Innatraea, who gave birth to the Three Sisters.

Asherah Tree (Ash-err-ah): An ancient mythological species of tree that is the symbol of Asherah. They are believed to have provided the seeds that gave birth to Innatraea.

Banque Dupris: The banque owned and operated by House Dupris throughout Innatraea's eastern region.

Basaraba (bass-r-ab-uh): A shepherd band leader, husband to Stevana, and father to Nicolai.

Bernard: Proprietor of the Feather and Quill inn in the river trade town Talberston's Crossing.

Beshim (besh-m): A young shepherd.

Bethseda (Beth-said-ah): The capital city of Aedonia.

The Bishop Family: A Cathyoran noble house.

Biume (Be-ohm): A Cathyoran royal servant who assists with the birthing and caring of the family's children.

Briallen Bishop (Bree-al-in) A baby Cathyoran girl, daughter of Ceridwen Bishop, twin sister to Eira Bishop, and heir to House Bishop.

Brianna Carlon (Bree-ahn-an kar-lawn): An older Cathyoran woman, Edmond's grandmother, and the last biume of House Ahearne.

Brighid (Breej): A Cathyoran woman, and member of Trefn Cyfiawnder. Bonded to the Dryad Nerthal, and wielder of the sword Gwreichionen. Mother of Aisling, and sister of Elspeth.

Brynn (Brin): The capital city of Cathyor, a cultural and political heartland until its destruction by Aedonia.

Byd Nesaf "Next World" (Beed ness-off): The Cathyoran afterlife, believed to be a spirit world where souls rest after death, often invoked in farewells like "Marw yn dda" (die well).

Byw yw marw, marw yw byw. "To live is to die, to die is to have lived." (B-yoo yoo mar-oo, mar-oo yoo b-oo): A Cathyoran soldier's saying.

Caleb: An Aedonian man, anointed of Jhoras, and Commander of a Jhorian Fist.

Calon (Kal-on): A Dryad, bonded to Elspeth Anwyl.

Cangen Marw "Dead Branch" (Kan-in mar-oo): A Trefn Cyfiawnder sword.

Caoimhe (Kwee-va): A Cathyoran woman, and an archer.

Cassian (Kass-ee-in): A venator who works for the Jhorians.

Catena "Witch's chain" (Kuh-tee-nuh): A special cloth band used by Jhorians to blind and deafen captured Weavers.

Cathyor (Kath-yore): One of the last ancient kingdoms. Conquered by Aedonia some years ago.

Ceridwen Bishop (Ke-rid-wen); A Cathyoran woman, member of Trefn Cyfiawnder, and last matriarch of House Bishop. Mother to Briallen and Eira Bishop.

Cian Ahearne (Kee-an ah-hear-nay): A baby Cathyoran boy, child of Isolde and Cormac Ahearne, and the last Prince heir of Cathyor.

Claudia Geisterschwert (Cloud-ee-ah gaist-ur-schwurt): Petra and Leonhard Geisterschwert's cousin.

Coedwig Amser "Forest of Time" (Kaid-wig ahm-ser): The abstract "forest" that is eons old and represents the ongoing sacred magical bond between the Dryads and the women of Trefn Cyfiawnder.

Coeden Gysegredig "Sacred Tree" (Kaid-en gai-seg-red-ig): The sacred emblem of Trefn Cyfiawnder, a tree-and-sword symbolizing the eternal bond between Cathyoran women and their Dryad allies.

Colin: A Cathyoran man.

Cormac Ahearne (Kor-mak ah-hear-nay): The last king of Cathyor, and last patriarch of House Ahearne. Husband to Queen Isolde Ahearne, father to Prince Cian Ahearne, and son of Taran Ahearne.

Crilla Sharone (Krill-ah share-ohn-ay): A retired Weaver of legendary status. Gertrude Al'Shane's sister. Crilla became Rosalie Sharone's adoptive mother after finding her abandoned as a baby.

Crogwyr, "Executioner" (Cog-wee-ah): Elspeth Anwyl's sword.

Crows: Nickname for the Jhorian Inquisitors.

Cyfeillach Gysegredig "Sacred Bond" (Kev-ah-shawk gai-seg-red-ig): The sacred magical bond between a woman of Trefn Cyfiawnder and her Dryad.

Cynddaredd "Fury" (Kin-dar-red): Isolde Ahearne's sword.

Cysgod "Shadow" (Kas-god): The spies and infiltrators of Trefn Cyfiawnder.

Danae (Dan-ay): The semi-nomadic people who inhabit the outskirts of the vast Tanglewood. They can also be found in small numbers throughout many other kingdoms.

Daphshire (Daf-shy-ur): A small region of vineyards north of Bethseda.

Daphshire Grand Ball: A semi-annual celebration held by vineyards in Daphshire for families of wealth and influence.

Daughters of Jhoras (Jo-ras): More often referred to as Confessors, they are women chosen by Jhoras to hear and forgive sins of the anointed.

Dduwies Rhyfel "Goddesses of War" (Du-we-es rav-el): The most elite warriors of Trefn Cyfiawnder.

Declan Cosgrove (Dek-luhn kos-grohv): A Cathyoran man, Captain of the Banque Dupris guard. Husband to Fiona Cosgrove.

Daphne (Daf-nee): The Dryad connected to the Great Tree known as the Shepherd King.

Diofrit (Di-oh-frit): A young woman working at the Drunken Bear Inn in the river trade town Talberston's Crossing.

Dryad: A Sacred Folk race. These giant feminine titans share a spiritual bond with Innatraea's Great Trees and are able to traverse between Innatraea and the spirit world known as Kanraphim.

The Dupris Family: A noble Aedonian House and owners of Banque Dupris.

Inquisitor Durand (Dur-and): An inquisitor of the Holy Church of Jhoras.

Dydd dial a Marwolaeth "Day of vengeance and death" (Deez dee-al ah mar-oo lai-eth): The prophesized day when Cathyor's fallen will rise to destroy the Jhorians and Aedonia.

Dygwr Tynged, "Fatebringer" (Dye-wee-ah Tin-yed): The Ahearne Family Sword, known to have a horse head-shaped pommel. Unique among Trefn Cyfiawnder swords because its magic can be used by a man of the Ahearne Family.

Dylan: A Cathyoran man, and a soldier.

Edmond Carlon (Ed-mond Car-lawn): Childhood friend to Rosalie and Jonaas, Brianna's grandson.

Edriel (Ed-ree-el): An Aedonian man, and an anointed of Jhoras.

Eira Bishop (Aye-ruh): A baby Cathyoran girl, daughter of Ceridwen Bishop, twin sister to Briallen Bishop, and heir to House Bishop.

Elspeth Anwyl (Els-peth ann-wh-eel): A Cathyoran woman, member of Trefn Cyfiawnder, sister of Brighid, and aunt of Aisling.

Emma: A woman working at the Drunken Bear Inn in the river trade town Talberston's Crossing.

Enoh (E-no): A shepherd.

Ethan: An Aedonian man, and an anointed of Jhoras.

Etheldreda (Eth-el-dree-duh): A Cathyoran woman, and a member of Trefn Cyfiawnder.

Feather and Quill: An inn in the river trade town Talberston's Crossing.

Fiona Cosgrove (fee-ohn-uh kos-grohv): A Cathyoran woman, wife to Declan Cosgrove, and a biume.

Fist of Jhoras, or Jhorian Fist (jo-ras, jo-ree-un): A military unit of anointed, generally consisting of twelve men and one commander.

Gertrude Al'Shane (Gur-true-de Al-sheyn): Jonaas' adoptive mother, wife to Jonathan, and sister to Crilla Sharone.

Gideon Ludheim (gid-ee-in lood-highm): An Aedonian man, anointed of Jhoras, and a knight.

Gisella (jee-zel-uh): Wife of Herbert, mother of Amelia and Sarai.

Glendid (glen-ded): Archibald Stallwood's horse.

Great Dryad/Dryad: A Sacred Folk race. Giant feminine titans, spirits of nature who appear to be half woman and half tree, bonded to Innatraea's Great Trees. The Dryads of Cathyor also share a bond with the women of Trefn Cyfiawnder.

Great Tree: The commonly used moniker referring to any of the ancient giant trees around Innatraea. Most have specific names and tower over their surroundings, whether near cities or even mountains.

Gregoire D'Arganse (greg-or d-r-gance): An Aedonian man, high king of Aedonia.

Gwarchodlu Brenhinol "Royal Guard" (gwar-hod-lee brin-heen-ol): A special unit within Trefn Cyfiawnder, the royal guard to the Cathyoran king.

Gwendolyn (gwen-dol-en): An older Cathyoran woman,

Gwr gweddw "Widowmaker" (gor gwen-or): The Bresling family sword.

Gwydir Wood (gwidd-eer): A forest in Cathyor.

Gwreichionen "Glimmer" (gresh-ee-ohn-en): Brighid's sword.

Hadriana (had-ree-on-ah): A Cathyor woman, and a member of Trefn Cyfiawnder.

Haversfjord (Hav-urs-fyord): A large Aedonian rivertrade town on the King's Highway.

Heimeric (hi-mer-ik): A man who works as the strongarm for the Drunken Bear Inn in the river trade town Talberston's Crossing. Husband to Mabel.

Herbert: Husband to Gisella, father to Amelia and Sarai.

The Holy Church of Jhoras (Jo-ras): The official church of Aedonia. It's known for its strong military, harsh judgments, political power, wealth, and hatred of those who challenge it. The Holy Church has a long history of oppressing women's power and violent conflicts with The Weavers.

Indila (in-dee-lah): A Cathyoran woman, and a member of Trefn Cyfiawnder.

Innatraea (Ee-nah-tray-uh): The known world.

Innatraean (Ee-nah-tray-uhn): The human folk of the known world.

Inquisitor: A special class within the anointed of Jhoras. Investigators, holders of holy relics, and questioners for the Holy Church of Jhoras.

Irmina (eer-meen-ah): Proprietress of the Drunken Bear Inn in the river town of Talberston's Crossing. Wife to the now deceased Nathanael.

Isolde Ahearne (eh-zuld-uh ah-hear-nay): A Cathyoran woman, wife to Cormac Ahearne, mother to Cian Ahearne, a member of Trefn Cyfiawnder, and Queen of Cathyor.

Jhoras (Jo-ras): The one God of the Holy Church of Jhoras.

Jhorian Crows (Jo-ree-an): The left arm, inquisitors and exorcists of the Holy Church of Jhoras.

Jhorian Phalanx (Jo-ree-an): The mighty right arm, or military, knights of the Holy Church of Jhoras.

Jonaas Al'Shane (Jo-nus Al-Sheyn): Childhood friend of Edmond and Rosalie.

Jonathan Al'Shane (Jaa-nuh-thn Al-Sheyn): Jonaas' adopted father, Gertrude's husband.

Kanraphim (Kan-ruh-fim): The spirit world and/or afterlife. The actual beliefs vary drastically between different kingdoms and peoples.

Kidner (Kid-nehr): A man who works for Reeve Stallwood in Haversfjord.

The King's Highway: The large, well-maintained, well-guarded trade road running through Aedonia. From the northern Jhorian coastal trade city Porto de ła Luce, through the kingdom's capital city of Bethseda, and all the way south to the border of Royal Seyla.

Lake Rhiannon (ree-an-non): The large lake, named after the goddess Rhiannon, in Cathyor by the capital city of Brynn.

Legacy: A new Weaver initiate who is sponsored by a current or retired Weaver. Many times, they are the sponsor's child.

Leonhard Geisterschwert (lee-on-hard gaist-ur-schwurt): Twin brother of Petra Geisterschwert, and cousin of Claudia Geisterschwert.

Lorna (lor-nah): A Cathyoran woman, and a member of Trefn Cyfiawnder.

Mabel (may-bel): A young woman who works at the Drunken Bear Inn in the river trade town Talberston's Crossing. Wife to Heimeric.

Marged Llewellyn (Mar-ged Luh-wel-in): One of the few survivors of Trefn Cyfiawnder. She lives in Aliselle Falls with her two husbands, Brandon and Rory. She helped train Edmond Carlon.

Martin: An Aedonian man, and an anointed of Jhoras.

Matilda: A woman working at the Drunken Bear Inn in the river trade town Talberston's Crossing.

Matos (mat-os): A shepherd.

Meabh Bresling (mayv bres-ling): A Cathyoran woman, mother of Morrigan Bresling, and a member of Trefn Cyfiawnder.

Merima (mare-eem-ah): A Cathyoran woman, and a member of Trefn Cyfiawnder.

Miniatura (min-ee-ah-tur-ah): Small figurines, representing noble houses or military units, used to plan military campaigns.

Morrigan Bresling (mohr-eh-gan bres-ling): A young Cathyoran girl. Best friend of Aisling, daughter of Meabh Bresling.

Nathanael (nathan-a-el); Deceased husband of Irmina.

Nerthal (neer-tal): A Dryad, bonded to Brighid.

Nicolai (nee-ko-lai): A young shepherd, son of Stevana and Basaraba.

Niomh (Nee-ohm): A Danae woman living on the streets of Haversfjord with her daughter Aife.

Oryvn (or-vin): A Cathyoran man.

Owain (ow-ain): A Cathyoran man, and a soldier.

Petra Geisterschwert (pet-rah gaist-ur-schwurt): Twin sister of Leonhard Geisterschwert, cousin of Claudia Geisterschwert.

Poen "Pain" (pyn): One of Marged Llewellyn's twin daggers.

Porto de la Luce, "Light's Port" (Por-toe-dey-lah-loos): Aedonia's large northern coastal trade city. Known as the seat of power of the Holy Church of Jhoras.

Pwerau Cysegredig "Sacred Power" (pw-air-igh sigh-seg-red-ig): A rare magical power that a woman of Trefn Cyfiawnder from the oldest bloodlines is sometimes born with.

Rheolaeth "Death" (ray-oh-lai-eth): One of Marged Llewellyn's twin daggers.

Rhiannon, the Great Horse Queen (Ree-an-non): One of the Three Sisters. Goddess of the moon, wealth, power, and fertility. Goddess of the Cathyoran people.

Rhosynd (Ross-end): A Dryad.

Rhyfelfeistr "Warmaster" (hav-vel-vay-stir): A title within Trefn Cyfiawnder, the woman responsible for training new recruits.

Rhys (rees): A Cathyor woman, and a member of Trefn Cyfiawnder.

Roots of Destiny: A phrase referring to a powerful destiny growing within, like tree roots.

Rosalie Sharone (Row-zuh-lee share-ohn-ay): Childhood friend of Jonnas and Edmond, adopted daughter and legacy of retired Weaver Crilla Sharone. As Crilla's Legacy, she is destined to join the Weavers on Sceotan.

Sacred Folk: The collective moniker for any of the ancient mythical non-Innatraean races of Innatraea. The actual number of different races and how many are still surviving is unknown. The many stories about their magical powers and origins vary greatly between regions and races.

Sarai (sar-ai): Daughter of Gisella and Herbert, sister of Amelia.

Sceotan (skay-oh-tan): Island kingdom of the Weavers. Located off the southern coast of Innatraea.

Sceotian (Skay-ocean): The native people of Sceotan.

Selene, The Moon Dog (Sell-een): One of the Three Sisters. Goddess of transition, roads, and the night.

Ser (Sehr): Honorific given to an Aedonian knight and lord.

Serafina, The Fire Snake (Sehrah-fee-nuh): One of the Three Sisters. Goddess of fire, light, passion, and rage.

Shepherd King: A great tree in Aedonia bordering the King's Highway.

Shatranj (Shuh-traanj): An ancient and very popular game of strategy played on a wooden board between two opponents.

Sica (si-ka): A dual-bladed knife carried by every anointed of Jhoras.

Sigridur (sig-rid-ur): A Cathyor woman, and a member of Trefn Cyfiawnder.

Stanislav (Stan-es-slav): An Aedonian man, a soldier, and servant to Aedonian high king Gregoire D'Arganse.

Stevana (Stev-ahn-ah): A shepherd, wife to Basaraba, and mother to Nicolai.

Styfnig (Stahv-nig): Elspeth Anwyl's horse.

Synnwyr y Galon 'Heart Sense" (Sen-wyr a gal-on): One of the Trefn Cyfiawnder Pwerau Cysegredig. The ability to sense when a woman ascends into their order through accepting Cyfeillach Gysegredig with a Dryad.

Talberston's Crossing (Tahl-burr-stuns): A river town in Aedonia.

Taran Ahearne (tar-ahn ah-hear-nay): A now deceased Cathyoran man, former King of Cathyor, and father to Cormac Ahearne.

Tavid the Traveler (Tav-eed): A book written by a man of the same name. The book details his many travels throughout Innatraea as well as cultural and historical information on nearly every kingdom and people, including the Sacred Folk.

Tawney (Tawn-ee): A horse that belongs to Gisella and Herbert.

Theo (Tay-oh): The town drunk of Talberston's Crossing.

Three Sisters (The daughters of Asherah): Rhiannon, Selene, and Seraphina. Innatraea's three sister goddesses and moons.

Toman (Toh-man): A shepherd.

Tomas (Toh-moss): A Cathyor man, servant to the Bresling family.

Trefn Cyfiawnder, "Order of Justice" (Trev-n Kuh-vyown-dehr): Cathyor's legendary women warriors. Who wield magic in battle connected to the Great Dryads.

Tytus (Ty-tus): An Aedonian man, an anointed of Jhoras, and Commander of a Jhorian Fist.

Venator "huntsman" (Ven-ee-tor): Woodsmen hired by various Aedonians as hunters, scouts, and trackers.

Victory River: The large river, big enough for ships to sail easily, spans Innatraea from north to south. Most of the river lies within Aedonia's borders.

The Weavers: An ancient organization made up of those who can Weave from all over Innatraea.

Weaving: The innate ability to see the threads of magical power that make up Innatraea and manipulate them at will. It is a rare trait few are born with.

Will of Jhoras (Jo-ras): Jhoras's Will and power enacted, or used, by his followers on Innatraea.

Novella Four Preview:
Verjin Paterazm
(The Last War)

ecades ago...

A sharp breeze blew over Jonathan, ruffling his cloak and sending a chill through his tunic. A common thing on the Sea of Grass. With nothing but flat plains for leagues, the wind gained strength over vast distances. The cold had been a hard lesson in the months since this campaign had begun, especially at night, when the air seemed to freeze like the emptiness of those endless plains. It often reminded him of an old saying from home: "Mae'r gwynt yn greulon i'r rhai sydd ar goll." The wind is cruel to those who are lost. Was he lost? Lately he felt that way, like shallow roots exposed to winter winds.

The wind and cold weren't the worst of it, though. Jonathan tightened his grip, feeling the tiredness in his hand and the stretch of his leather glove over his sword's pommel. He rubbed his eyes. It was becoming harder of late to make himself focus on the war and camp matters, when all he really wanted to do was leave with Gertrude.

A new battalion of young recruits had arrived from Brynn a few weeks ago. They had been escorted by a Trefn Cyfiawnder warrior named Scatha Cadain, a woman whose reputation preceded her. She was known as a brash and skilled combatant, with a particularly boisterous—some would say even bawdy—sense of humor and temperament. He'd met her and knew she was a very skilled warrior, but she definitely took some getting used to. Then again, that was the case with most women from Trefn Cyfiawnder. They were powerful, and they knew it. One of them came to check on things here every few months. This campaign was important to them because its purpose was to secure the last major trade route between Cathyor and the Rinowhn Tribes.

Jonathan shook himself, shifting his attention to the young soldier talking to him. Phylip had arrived with those recruits. The man still looked like a boy to Jonathan. But this was war. You aged quickly, and those who didn't learn fast died. The months they'd been out here already felt like years to him—that was just the way of things.

"What did you say, lad? How many?"

The boy cleared his throat and spoke louder, assuming Jonathan couldn't hear him. He hadn't been here long enough to know the look of a man lost in his own thoughts. "Three, Ser, all from Mynydd."

Jonathan looked towards a disturbance at the defensive line, but it was just a new train of Ta'juo supply wagons arriving, brimming with sacks of grain and bundled trade goods. "Mynydd? Isn't that where you're from?"

Phylip's eyes carried the weight every new soldier learned too soon. "Yes, Ser, it is."

"Did you know them?"

"Yes, Ser, we all grew up there and enlisted together, too."

Jonathan put a hand on the boy's shoulder and squeezed. "I'm sorry, lad. But they're with Rhiannon now. She'll look after their souls." He met the boy's eyes, holding their attention. "Bydded iddynt ddod o hyd i heddwch yn y Byd Nesaf." May they find peace in the next world.

Phylip wiped his eyes and dipped his head. "Bydded iddynt ddod o hyd i heddwch yn y Byd Nesaf." Thank you, Ser.

The boy needed something to do—a soldier required a task. "Go check on those new supply wagons.Help Master Tegid account for everything."

"Yes, Ser."

Jonathan didn't really expect any duplicity from their Rinowhn allies, but supplies were scarce and it was best to keep an eye on things. He watched the boy go as Phylip headed toward the wagons, fading into the bustling throng. Then he turned, scanning the camp, its rhythm a soldier's pulse: clashing steel, shouted orders, the creak of Ta'juo wagons. I'okanew laughter, sharp and mocking, drifted from the blacksmith's tent.

When he and the other Cathyorans had first come here the Rinowhn had taken some getting used to. But that was the purpose of this campaign, to help their Rinowhn Tribe allies resist the Aedonian advance into their homeland, thus securing Cathyor's last trade route. At first

Jonathan hadn't understood why, but now he did. When you had a relentless enemy like Aedonia, and the Holy Church of Jhoras, you made alliances with anyone you could. War made for strange friendships.

As if on cue with Jonathan's thoughts, one of the dark-skinned I'okanew men slapped another on the back. "Isando Esikhulu."

Both men smirked at the joke as the group kept walking.

Jonathan knew those words now; they meant "Big Hammer," a phrase they used to refer to his childhood friend Deitrich, who was one of the camp's blacksmiths. It sounded harmless enough, even respectful, but over time he had come to know better. The I'okanew language often had multiple meanings, like parables, opposites, or insinuations. Jonathan could still remember the first time he'd figured this out, learning their tongue's cunning. They had called another soldier umgijimi osheshayo, which meant "fast runner," but what they were really calling the man was "chicken," because he'd run from the enemy; they didn't care that the man had been vastly outnumbered and alone.

In this case having a "Big Hammer" also meant the blacksmith was a small man. The name had caught on after Deitrich's first engagement, when he had quit being a soldier and decided to be a blacksmith like his father.

Truthfully, he much preferred the other Rinowhn war party with them. The Ta'al were more respectful in their attitude towards others. They also fielded women warriors, which echoed his people's women soldiers and the knights of Trefn Cyfiawnder. Many of the men enjoyed gazing upon the Ta'al women, a muscular tan-skinned woman wielding the vicious Ta'al bullwhip was something to behold. It also helped that their expert hunting and scouting kept everyone well fed. They were a sharp contrast to the sarcastically cruel spear- and shield-wielding I'okanew men.

Jonathan walked over to the blacksmith's tent after the I'okanew men walked on. "Hey there, small man."

Deitrich chuckled as he looked up from plunging a red-hot glowing sword blade into a barrel of oil. It hissed as he set his tongs down before speaking. "You have your own name too, tree boy. Need I remind you?"

Jonathan leaned against a nearby post and held his hands up. "No need for that."

Deitrich beamed and rubbed his chin. "What was it now?" He made a great show of trying to remember something, even though he knew it exactly. "Ah yes, inkemba yehlathi. It means 'sword of the forest,' right?"

Truthfully, his name was an even bigger joke than Deitrich's. They were both Cathyoran, and forests were sacred. But in this case the "forest" was all their soldiers and being one of their swords meant he was only as good as any implement a soldier could grab off a weapons rack.

Jonathan rolled his eyes. "Thank you for the reminder."

Deitrich inclined his head, as if he'd done his friend a favor. He grabbed the sword again with his tongs. "Did more oil arrive today? We're getting low again."

Jonathan nodded. "We should know soon. The wagons just arrived and I sent a soldier to help Tegid inventory them."

"Thank you." Deitrich smirked conspiratorially. "Did you find a ring?"

Jonathan crossed his arms, his demeanor becoming thoughtful. "I did. The last caravan of Ta'juo had some beautiful lapis pieces. I was able to trade for one that's suitable."

Jonathan glanced around carefully, making sure they were alone before taking the ring from his pocket and holding it up. The sun glinted off its blue and gold contours, making it glow. He knew that Gertrude would love it.

Deitrich whistled. "That's a pretty piece alright. When are you going to ask her?"

Jonathan put the ring away and looked around again. "Soon, I think—maybe even today. It's time."

"What will you do if she says yes? Gertrude doesn't strike me as a woman who will be happily married to a soldier."

Jonathan smirked. "She isn't at that. I think it's time for me to make some more decisions, too, my friend." He sighed. "I've been thinking about taking my pension and retiring, maybe buying a small farm."

"You've thought a lot about this."

"Indeed, my friend. I'm tired. I don't want to fight anymore."

Deitrich set the sword aside and took his heavy gloves off, then came to stand closer. "You know, Emilia recently asked me if we could leave, too."

Jonathan raised an eyebrow at his friend. "Did she?"

Deitrich crossed his arms and nodded. "Aye. Maybe it's time for all of us to make some changes."

Jonathan inclined his head, understanding. "Do you think the army will suffer because of our absence?"

Deitrich paused, then placed his hands on Jonathan's shoulders. "They have an entire kingdom of women and men willing to fight. We're Cathyoran. It's our choice!"

Jonathan agreed. "Aye, that's true, old friend. I think that I need to go see Gertrude. Mae'n bryd siarad ä thynged." It's time to speak with fate.

To the community that helped make Innatraea possible, thank you.

Peter, Vesna, Manca, Julija, GiGi, Pouchi, Jeanine, Jean-Paul, Fil, Hétu, Irak, Marian M., George M., Todd M., Jason Bratt, Justin Bratt, C.M., Spencer P., Moriah C., Vanessa C., Brandon H. Westmoreland, Jim Chabot, Anne Chabot, Samantha Hopkins, Ron, Elaine, John, Justin, Jacob, Lori Crutchfield, Dusty Ranger, Michael B., Dawne M. Mitchell, Nathaniel L. Glenn, Lincoln Escandon, G. Reyes, Sam J., N.C., Michael Kantor,

Learn more about Innatraea!

www.innatraea.com

About the Author

E.R. Zaugg is a neurodivergent poet, novelist, and parent whose work transforms personal experience into speculative theology. A lifelong traveler and student of global spiritual traditions—from Catholic mysticism to Kabbalistic cosmology to Buddhist philosophy to Pagan earth wisdom—he weaves insights from vulnerable cultures into fantasy that centers those historically erased from epic narratives.

His award-winning poetry and essays on raising a trans child draw from the conviction that choice, freedom, and universal rights matter more than any system that would deny them. As a single father from Seattle, he learned that the smallest acts of love create ripples powerful enough to reshape destinies—a truth that pulses through every page of his work.

The Innatraea series, beginning with Small Footsteps, reimagines epic fantasy through cultures inspired by Welsh, Armenian, Cherokee, Romani, and other peoples whose stories deserve cosmic significance. Each novella in the saga asks: what if the vulnerable weren't just survivors, but the prophetic center of creation itself? Through magic systems rooted in consent, warrior orders bonded to ancient trees, and immortal beings facing extinction, Zaugg crafts poetic prose that refuses to simplify power, trauma, or hope.

Dedicated to his child Siri, who taught him that creativity weaves dreams into reality, his books invite readers to embrace a deeper, more complicated love of humanity—one that honors both the weight of suffering and the radical possibility of restoration.